HEIDI

Heidi is one of the world's classic children's stories. An orphan, left with her strange old grandfather who lived high up in the mountains, Heidi learned to love the mountains, the strange old man who looked after her so tenderly, his goats, the goat boy and the people of the little village who became her friends.

Then one day she was taken to Frankfurt, to become the companion of a sick girl. It was a beautiful home, but apart from Klara, the people were strange and unfriendly until Klara's grandmother taught Heidi how to deal with them. But Heidi pined for her beloved mountains, and it was when she returned there, and Klara and her grandmother came to stay, that they worked their magic on Klara too, restoring her to health and strength.

Heidi is in the great tradition of child heroines, and her story is as popular today as it was when it was written more than a hundred years ago.

HEIDI

BY

JOHANNA SPYRI

SCHOLASTIC INC.

New York Toronto London Auckland Sydney

ISBN 0-590-33936-2

12 11 10 9 8 7 6 5 4 3 2   6 7 8 9/8 0/9

Printed in the U.S.A.   01

CONTENTS

Part I: HEIDI'S YEARS OF LEARNING

Part II: HEIDI USES WHAT SHE LEARNED

PART I

Heidi's Years of Learning

Chapter 1

UP TO THE ALM-UNCLE

FROM the pleasant village of Mayenfeld a path leads through green fields, richly covered with trees, to the foot of the mountain, which from this side majestically overhangs the valley. Where the path grows steeper, and goes straight up to the Alps, the perfume of sweet mountain plants welcomes the traveller.

Along this steep mountain path a sturdy, wholesome girl climbed one clear, sunny morning in June, leading by the hand a child whose cheeks flamed as if an inner fire glowed through her sunburned skin. And little wonder, for the child was as bundled up on this sunny June morning as if she were to be protected from a bitter frost. She could be scarcely more than five years old; but it was impossible to judge her size or shape, for she had on two, if not three, dresses, one on top of the other. And over all, wound round and round, was a long red woollen scarf.

The lumpy figure, with its heavy hobnailed mountain shoes, toiled, hot and weary, up the steep hillside. After an hour's climb from the valley, the two girls reached the hamlet of Dorfli, halfway up the Alm Mountain. Here they were greeted from almost every doorway and along the street, for the older girl had now reached her home town. However, without once stopping, she answered all questions and greetings as she swung along, until they reached the end of the hamlet, where only a few scattered cottages stood. Here someone called from a doorway: "Wait a minute, Dete, I will go with you if you are going farther." As Dete stood still, the child pulled loose and sat down on the ground.

"Are you tired, Heidi?" asked her companion.

"No, but I'm hot," replied the child.

"We are almost there. Try to hold out a little while longer. Take big steps, and in an hour we'll be there," Dete promised. A large, kindly woman came from a doorway to join the pair. The little girl fell in behind the two women who were deep in conversation about Dorfli people.

"Now, where are you taking the child, Dete?" asked the newcomer. "She's your sister's child, isn't she — the little orphan?"

"Yes, she is," said Dete. "I am taking her up to her grandfather's. She'll have to stay with him."

"What! Leave this child with the Alm-Uncle? You're out of your head, Dete. How can you even think of such a thing? He'll soon set you straight!"

"No, no, Barbel. He is her grandfather, and he has to do his share. I've looked after Heidi up to this time, and now I have a chance of a job that I can't pass up because of this child. Her grandfather simply has to take over."

"Yes, if he were like other people, Dete," rejoined Barbel anxiously. "But you know how he is. What's he going to do with a child? Such a young one, too! It won't work. But where are you planning to go?"

"To Frankfurt," explained Dete, "where I've been offered a really good place. The family was at the Baths last summer. I took care of their rooms in the hotel, and looked after their comfort so well that they wanted to take me back with them then. Now they have come again, they still want me, and I mean to accept this time."

"I wouldn't want to be that child," said Barbel, shaking her head. "No one knows how he lives up there. He has nothing to do with anybody, year in year out. He never sets foot in church. And when he comes down here once a year, with that heavy stick of his, everyone is afraid of him and keeps out of his way. With his bushy grey eyebrows, and his frightful beard, he looks so like a wild man that people hope they won't meet him alone."

"Just the same," insisted Dete, "he is the grandfather, and he has to take care of the child. He won't hurt her. Anyhow, I'm through."

"I certainly would like to know," Barbel speculated, "what that old man has on his conscience. He always looks around so suspiciously, and he lives all alone up there on the Alm, hiding like a hermit. People say all sorts of queer things about him, but you must know the truth from your sister. Don't you, Dete?"

"Yes, but I'm not telling because if he ever thought I had said anything, I'd get what-for!"

But Barbel had long wanted to know why the Alm-Uncle had lived alone on the mountain top; and why people spoke so cautiously about him, as if they could not say anything favourable, and would not speak against him. Neither did Barbel know why everybody in Dorfli called the old man Alm-Uncle. He could not be the real uncle of all the inhabitants; but as they always called him so, she did, too.

Because Barbel had been married only a short time, and had come from the village of Prattigau after her wedding, she did not yet know all the ins and outs of life in Dorfli, nor the peculiarities of the people there or in the region. Her good friend Dete, however, had been born in Dorfli, and had lived there until her mother's death; then she had gone to Ragatz Bad, to work in the big hotel as chambermaid, at very good pay.

That very morning Dete had come with the child from Ragatz; a friend had given them a ride in his hay cart as far as Mayenfeld. Barbel longed to learn a little more. She laid her hand confidentially on her friend's arm, saying: "Dete, you can tell me the real truth about the Alm-Uncle. I don't believe half that people here say. Do tell me. What's wrong with the old man? And has everyone always been afraid of him? Has he always seemed to hate his fellow beings as he does now?"

"Whether he has always been like this, I can't say, since I'm just twenty-six years old, and he is at least seventy. So don't ask me to tell you how he was when he was young. If I could only be sure that what I tell you wouldn't be spread around in Prattigau, I might give you an earful. My mother and he both came from Domleschg."

"Oh, Dete!" replied Barbel, reproachfully, "what do you mean? We aren't all blabbermouths in Prattigau, after all. I can keep a secret, if necessary. So go on and tell me, do. You won't be sorry."

"Well, I will. But mind you keep your word," Dete warned. She looked back, to see if the child were near enough to overhear what they said, but Heidi was nowhere in sight. She had ceased following some time earlier, but they had been too busy talking to notice her absence. Dete stopped, and looked about in every direction. The path made one or two curves, but yet the eye could follow it almost down to Dorfli. There was no one visible for its whole length.

"I see her now!" exclaimed Barbel. "Down there, don't you see her?" and she pointed to a spot quite distant from the mountain path. "She is climbing up the cliff with Peter, the goatherd, and his flock. I wonder why he is so late today? It is lucky for us, for you can go on with your story while he looks after the child."

"Peter won't need to put himself out much, looking after her," said Dete. "She uses her own eyes, and sees everything that goes on. I have found that out, and it's good that she is bright. The old man will never be able to provide much for her. All he has are his two goats and the Almhut."

"Did he ever have more?" asked Barbel.

"Oh, my, yes!" replied Dete emphatically. "He used to have the very best farm in Domleschg. He was the eldest son, and had only one brother, who was quiet and steady.

4

But Alm-Uncle was a playboy and ran around with bad company. He gambled away every bit of his property, and when they found out, his father and then his mother died of mortification. His brother had nothing of course, and he moved away somewhere, out of humiliation. And since Alm-Uncle had nothing left but a bad name, *he* disappeared. At first, no one knew where he had gone, but after a while the word went around that he had joined the army, and gone to Naples. Then nobody heard anything for twelve years or more. All at once he showed up in Domleschg, with a half-grown boy, and tried to get his kinfolks to take them in. When he found every door closed against him, he became embittered and swore he would never set foot in Domleschg again. So he came to Dörfli. He lived here with his boy, maybe he still had a little money, because he gave Tobias, his son, a trade. Tobias was a nice fellow, a carpenter, and well liked by everyone in Dörfli. But nobody trusted the old man. People said that he had deserted from Naples, got in a brawl, and killed someone. But anyhow we recognized the relationship, because my great-grandmother and his mother were sisters; so we called him Uncle. Since we are related to everybody in Dörfli, on our father's side, gradually everybody called him Uncle; and when he moved on the Alm, everyone called him Alm-Uncle."

"But what happened to Tobias?" said Barbel, eagerly.

"Wait, I am coming to that. I can't tell you everything at once.

"Tobias went to learn his trade in Mels, and when he finished he returned to Dörfli, and married my sister, Adelheid, whom he had always liked. They got along fine, but, two years later, as Tobias was helping build a house, a beam fell on him and killed him. The shock, and sorrow, gave Adelheid a fever from which she never recovered. Strong and hearty as she had been, she went into a coma, so that you could not tell if she were waking or asleep. Two months after Tobias's death we buried Adelheid.

"Everybody talked about the sad fate of this couple, and

they said that it was a judgment on the Uncle for his godless life. Our pastor, appealing to his conscience, told him that he should come to church, but he just glowered and spoke to no one. Finally everyone avoided him. Next we heard, he had gone up to the Alm. Never coming down, he lived withdrawn from God and man.

"When Mother and I took Adelheid's little girl, Heidi, to live with us, she was a year old. Then, after Mother died, I decided to go to the Baths to work; I boarded Heidi at old Ursel's in Pfafferserdorf. I was able to stay at the Baths all winter, for there was plenty of sewing and mending for me to do. As I told you, the family I worked for last year came back from Frankfurt early this spring, and they still want to take me back with them. I am going, day after tomorrow, and it's a fine job, believe me."

"And you'll leave that child up there with the old man." I can't understand what you are thinking of, Dete," Barbel shook her head reproachfully.

"What do you mean?" snapped Dete. "I've done my share for the child, and what else can I do? I can't drag along a five-year-old to Frankfurt with me. Now where are you going, Barbel? Here we are already halfway up to the Alm."

"I've reached the place I want," said Barbel. "I have to speak to the mother of Peter, the goatherd. She spins for me in the winter. So goodbye, Dete! Good luck to you!"

Dete shook hands with her companion. She stood watching Barbel go toward the small dark brown cottage which stood a little way off the main path. Built in a sheltered hollow, halfway up the Alm, the house was so ramshackle and weatherbeaten that – exposed to the fierce mountain winds – it seemed a dangerous dwelling.

Indeed, it looked as if it might be swept down into the valley at any time. Here lived Peter, the eleven-year-old boy whose business it was to drive the goats from Dorfli, every morning, up on the Alm, to let them crop the short, succulent bushes that grew there. In the evening he led his nimble-footed herd down into Dorfli again and gave a shrill whistle on his fingers as a signal to the owners to come to the little square and get their goats. Usually, little boys and girls came for the animals, for such gentle creatures could do them no harm. All summer long, this was the only time of day when Peter was with young companions. All the rest of the time he spent alone with his goats.

To be sure, he had the company of his mother and his blind grandmother; but he left the hut early in the morning, and returned late from Dorfli. Because he wanted to play with the children as long as possible, he spent only enough time at home to swallow his bread and milk.

His father, who also had been called goat-Peter, had been killed while felling trees the year before. His mother, whose name was Brigitte, was always spoken of as goat-Peterin, or goat-Peter's mother, and "Grandmother" was what everybody, far and near, called his blind grandmother.

Dete stood waiting for a full ten minutes, looking in every direction for the children and the goats, who again were nowhere to be seen. Then, impatiently, she climbed still higher to get a better view of the valley, searching in every direction.

In the meantime, the children had gone a roundabout way. Peter knew of many spots where there were all sorts of fine bushes and herbs for his goats to nibble. To reach these, he wandered from one place to another with his flock. At first Heidi laboriously climbed after him. Encumbered by her heavy wraps, she was obliged to exert all her little strength just to keep going.

She said nothing, however, but studied first Peter, who, with his bare feet and light trousers, sprang here and there without the least trouble; and then the goats, with their thin, slender legs, climbing still more easily over bushes and stones, and even up the precipices. Suddenly Heidi sat down and pulled off her shoes and stockings. Up again, she threw off the thick woollen scarf; then, unfastening the buttons on her top dress, she flung it away, and began

7

undoing the next one. To avoid carrying the clothes, Dete had put on all the child's Sunday things over her everyday garments. In a twinkling Heidi tore off her everyday dress too, and stood in her petticoat, delightedly stretching her bare arms out of the short sleeves of her little undershirt into the cooling wind.

Then she folded all her clothes into a neat pile and scrambled after the goats to Peter.

Peter had not noticed what the child was doing while she stayed behind, but when she came up beside him in her new costume he grinned. Then as he looked back and saw the little heap of clothes, his grin broadened, but he said nothing.

Now that Heidi felt herself so free and comfortable, she began to talk to the boy, and he had to answer all sorts of questions. How many goats had he? Where was he taking them, and what did he do when he reached his destination? At last, however, the children and the goats reached the hut, and Aunt Dete caught sight of them.

As soon as she saw her niece, she shouted, "Whatever have you been doing, Heidi? What have you done with your two dresses? And the shawl? And the new shoes that I bought you for the mountain? Where are the new stockings I knitted for you myself? Are they all gone? What have you done with them all?"

Heidi pointed down the mountainside. "There," she said.

Dete looked. Down below she saw something – and on the top of it was a spot of red. Was that the scarf?

"You mischievous girl!" cried Dete. "Why have you taken your clothes off? What does it mean?"

"I don't need them," Heidi replied, and did not look the least bit sorry for what she had done.

"Oh, you thoughtless child!" Dete scolded. "Who is to go for them now? It will take at least half-an-hour. Peter, do run down and fetch them for me. Well, don't stand there staring, as if you were nailed to the earth."

"I am late already," Peter replied, not stirring from the spot, and with his hands in his pockets, just as he'd stood when Dete's cries had first reached him.

"Come now, you shall have something nice for your trouble," Dete coaxed. "Do you see this?" She showed him a shining new coin.

Instantly he ran down the mountain, taking the shortest way, and reached the clothes in great strides. He scooped them up, and was back again so quickly that Dete had to praise him and give him the promised coin without delay. Peter thrust it deep into his pocket, his face beaming with pleasure, for a treasure like this rarely fell to his lot.

"You can carry the things for us up to Alm-Uncle's. You are going that way, I believe," said Dete, while she applied herself to climbing the path that rose steeply behind the goatherd's hut. He followed her willingly, carrying the bundle under his left arm, while he swung his rod with his right.

Heidi and the goats leaped about joyfully in every direction.

Thus the small procession at last reached the summit of the Alm, after three-quarters of an hour's climbing. There stood the old uncle's hut, exposed to all the winds of heaven, but taking advantage of every ray of sunlight, and commanding a most beautiful view of the valley.

Behind the hut grew three very old pine trees, with long, thick branches. Then the mountain rose up and up to the old grey rocks, first over slopes covered with succulent herbs, then through thickly strewn boulders. At last came the bald, steep cliffs.

On the side of his hut overlooking the valley, Alm-Uncle had put a bench. Here he sat now. His pipe was in his mouth and his hands rested on his knees as he watched the children, the goats, and Aunt Dete clambering up the slope.

Heidi reached the summit first, and went directly to the old man. Stretching out her hand, she said, "Good evening, Grandfather."

"Well! And what does this mean?" answered the Alm-Uncle, his voice harsh. However, he gave his hand to the small girl and looked at her with a steady piercing gaze from under great bushy eyebrows.

Heidi returned his look with equal steadiness. What a strange-looking man was this grandfather of hers, with his long beard, and his grey eyebrows growing together in the middle. She had never seen anyone like him.

Meanwhile, Peter and Dete came to stand beside Heidi, Peter staying on to see what would happen.

"Good day, Uncle," said Dete. "I have brought you Tobias and Adelheid's child, whom you have not seen since she was just a year old."

"And what is this child to do with me?" demanded the old man. "You there!" he gestured to Peter, "move along with your goats. You are late! Take mine with you."

Peter jumped to obey. No one argued with Alm-Uncle.

"The child is to stay here with you," Dete began in a firm voice, "I have done my duty by her for four years. It's your turn now."

"Indeed!" roared the old man, his eyes flashing, "and if she starts to cry and whimper for you, what am I to do then?"

"That is your affair," Dete said. "No one told me what to do with her when she was thrust upon me – a year-old mite. What with my mother and myself to look after, I had my hands full already. Now I must go my way, and you are Heidi's next of kin. If you don't want to keep her, do what you please with her. Whatever happens to her is your business now."

For all her blustering, Dete's conscience was not easy, and she was working herself up into a temper, saying much more than she really meant. At her last words, Alm-Uncle stood up. He looked at her so strangely that she retreated a couple of steps.

"Go right on back where you came from," he shouted, "and don't come round any more."

Dete wasted no time. "Goodbye then – and to you, too, Heidi," she said, and ran down the mountainside without stopping, until she reached Dorfli. In Dorfli, people called to her and tried to stop her, for they all were curious to know what had become of the child. They knew Dete well, and they knew whose child Heidi was, too. "Where is the little girl? What have you done with the young one, Dete?" they called from doors and windows.

"Up there with the Alm-Uncle," she shouted back impatiently, without stopping.

But she was not comfortable about the situation. Everybody seemed too shocked. "How could you do it?" "The poor, poor little thing! How could you leave that helpless child up there?" All through the town horrified voices pursued her. "The poor tot!" "Poor motherless soul."

Dete raced on, and soon was beyond the reach of their voices. But her mind was troubled, for her mother, as she lay dying, had entrusted this grandchild, Heidi, to Dete. She tried to still her conscience by telling herself that she could do more for the child once she was in her fine new job. Nevertheless, she was glad to get away as quickly as possible from the questions and reproaches of her old friends.

Chapter 2

AT THE GRANDFATHER'S

WHEN Dete had left them, the old man sat down on his bench once more. Blowing great clouds of smoke from his pipe, he stared silently at the ground.

Heidi looked about her curiously. Discovering the goatshed, she peeped in, but it was empty, so she went on with her investigations. Finally she ran behind the hut to look at the great old pines.

The wind seemed to sing through the branches. Heidi stood listening, enchanted. But when the wind grew still, she went back to her grandfather. He sat as she had left him. Planting herself directly in front of the old man, she put her small hands behind her back and stared at him.

After a few moments he raised his head. "What do you want?" he asked.

"I want to see what you have there, in the hut," said Heidi.

"Well then, take up your things and come with me," her grandfather said, rising from the bench.

"I don't want them any more," the child said.

The old man turned to inspect his small granddaughter. Her black eyes were dancing with expectation.

"She's bright enough," he murmured to himself. To her he said. "Why don't you want them, child?"

"Because I want to go about like the goats," said Heidi, "to run as they do."

"And so you shall," replied her grandfather. "Bring your things in, anyway, and we will put them away." She picked up the bundle of clothes and followed him into the one large room which was the entire hut.

The bed was in one corner; in another a big kettle hung

over the hearth. There was also a table and a chair. In the wall was a door. This the grandfather opened to show a large cupboard. There he hung his clothes. On the shelves were shirts, stockings, handkerchiefs, cups, plates, saucers, and glasses. Above him the smoked meat, cheese and a round loaf of bread were set within easy reach. While he held the door open, Heidi stepped up with her bundle of clothes, which she stuffed in behind her grandfather's things, as far out of sight as possible. Then she turned and looked carefully about the room.

"Where shall I sleep, Grandfather?"

"Wherever you wish," he answered.

Pleased, Heidi ran about the room, inspecting every corner, to find the place that would suit her. Near her grandfather's bed stood a ladder which led into the hayloft. Heidi climbed right up and found the loft heaped with fresh, sweet-smelling hay. From a round hole in the rafters she found she could look far down into the valley.

"I'll sleep here!" she cried. "It's beautiful. Do come up, Grandfather, and see how beautiful it is here."

"That I know," he answered from below.

"I shall make my bed here," Heidi said, working busily away, "but you must bring me a sheet. There must be a sheet on my bed."

"Well, now," replied her Grandfather. Going to the cupboard, he searched about, and finally pulled out from under his shirts a long, coarse linen cloth. It might serve as a sheet.

He mounted the ladder with it, and found the hay piled neatly into the shape of a small bed with the head purposely high, so that from it one could look straight through the round open window.

That is well done," said the old man. "Now we'll put on the sheet, but first –" He took up great armfuls of hay, piling the bed up until it was twice as thick as Heidi had made it. Now she would not feel the hard floor through the hay. "Bring on the sheet," he directed Heidi.

She seized the sheet, but the linen was heavy – and that, of course, was good, for the hay could not get through such thickness. They both spread this sheet over the hay, and Heidi busily tucked it under. Now the bed looked neat and trim, and Heidi stood back to study it thoughtfully. "We have forgotten something, Grandfather," she said at last.

"What is that?"

"A coverlet! When one goes to bed, one must have a coverlet."

"But I have none," he said.

"Oh – well, that's all right," Heidi shrugged. "I'll just get more hay instead." She ran to fetch it, but her grandfather stopped her.

"Wait," he said. He went down the ladder, and over to his bed. Climbing up once more, he placed a heavy linen sack on the floor. "Isn't this better than hay?" he asked.

Heidi tugged at the sack, but she could not manage the heavy stuff. However, with the grandfather's help, it was soon properly arranged, and then the bed looked so nice that Heidi stood entranced.

"It's a perfect bed!" she said. "I wish it were night and bedtime already."

"We might have something to eat first," he suggested. "What do you think?"

Heidi had been so interested in her bed that she had forgotten everything else. Now she suddenly felt very hungry, for she'd eaten nothing since breakfast. And then she'd had only a piece of bread and a little weak coffee. Not much preparation for a long journey. Now she replied heartily to her grandfather's question, "Yes, I think we should."

"Let's go down then," the old man said, and followed her on the ladder.

At the fireplace, he moved the big kettle aside and hung a smaller one in its place on the chain. Then he seated himself on the three-legged stool and blew the fire until there was a good blaze. Soon the kettle began to boil. Now he held a long iron fork over the fire, with a big piece of cheese speared upon it. This he turned slowly around and around until it became golden yellow.

Heidi watched him, fascinated. Suddenly she had an idea and she ran to the cupboard, then back again to the table many times. When her grandfather brought the pot, and the toasted cheese on the fork to the table, the round loaf, two plates, and two knives, were already there, all neatly arranged. Heidi had noticed everything in the cupboard and she knew exactly what was needed for the meal.

"Now this is nice, that you can think of things yourself," the old man said, putting the cheese upon the bread. "But there is still something lacking."

The pot was steaming so invitingly, Heidi knew what was wanted, and dashed to the cupboard again. She found only one mug, but two glassess stood behind it. She soon returned with a glass and the mug.

"Very good. You are helpful. Now, where will you sit?" Grandfather asked, for he occupied the only high stool himself. Like an arrow Heidi sped back to the fireplace and returned with the little three-legged stool.

Grandfather nodded. "Now you have a seat," he said, "even though it is rather low. However, you would be too short, even on mine, to reach the table, still; you must have something to eat, so begin."

He rose, filled the mug with milk and set it upon the high stool. This he drew up to Heidi so that she had a table to herself. Seating himself on the corner of the table, Grandfather began to eat his dinner also.

Heidi seized the mug and drank and drank without stopping once. All the thirst of her journey seemed to come up at once. Then she drew a long breath and set down her mug.

"Is the milk good?" asked her grandfather.

"I never drank such good milk," Heidi said.

"You must have more, then," he said, filling the mug to the top. Heidi was now eating her bread, spread thickly with the hot cheese. It was soft as butter from the heat, and tasted delicious. She looked perfectly happy.

When they had finished, the old man went out to the goats' shed to put things to rights there. Heidi watched him carefully. First he swept everything up with the broom; then he strewed fresh straw about for the animals to sleep upon. Next he went to the woodpile near by and cut heavy round sticks of the right size and a board to the right shape. He bored holes in it, fitted the sticks in, and it suddenly became a stool like his own, only higher. Heidi was speechless with wonder.

"Do you know what this is, Heidi?" he asked.

"It must be my stool, because it's so high. How fast you make it!" she exclaimed.

"She knows what she sees," the old man said to himself, as he moved around the hut, driving in a nail here, making something fast there, going with his hammer and nails and pieces of wood from one place to another, constantly finding something to do, or to mend. Heidi followed his every step, watching everything that he did with complete attention, for everything that happened interested her.

Evening came at last. The wind sighed through the old trees. As it blew harder, the branches swayed back and forth. Heidi felt the sounds not only in her ears, but in her heart, and she was so happy that she ran out under the pines and leaped about for sheer joy.

Her grandfather stood in the doorway and watched the child.

Suddenly a shrill whistle sounded. Heidi stood still, and the old man stepped out. Down the mountain streamed the goats, one after the other, with Peter in their midst.

With a shout Heidi rushed into the flock, to greet her old friends of the morning.

Reaching the hut, all the animals stopped, and from out of the herd came two beautiful slender goats, one white and one brown. They went to the old man and licked his hands, for he held a small quantity of salt for them every evening as a welcome when they came home. Peter moved on with his flock. Heidi stroked Grandfather's goats gently; one, then the other. Next she ran to the other side, and did the same, delighted with the charming creatures.

"Are they both ours, Grandfather? Will they go into our shed? Will they always stay with us?" Heidi's questions rushed out in her excitement, with Grandfather scarcely given a chance to answer.

"Yes, child. Yes, yes." When the goats had licked up all the salt, Grandfather said, "Fetch me your little mug and some bread."

Heidi obeyed, and Grandfather first milked the goats into the mug, and then cut bits of bread and dropped them in.

"Now eat your supper, and go to bed," he said. "Dete left another bundle for you with your night clothes and other things. You'll find them in the cupboard. I must care for the goats now. So sleep soundly."

"Good night, Grandfather!" Heidi shouted after him, as he vanished with the goats. "What are their names, Grandfather?"

"The white one is Schwänli, the other Bärli," he called back.

"Good night, Schwänli! Good night, Bärli!" shouted Heidi at the top of her voice.

With the goats gone, she sat down on the bench to eat her bread and milk, but the wind grew so strong that it almost blew her off her seat. She ate as fast as she could, went into the cottage, and climbed up to her bed. She no sooner stretched out than she was fast asleep, and she slept all night as comfortably as a princess in a palace.

Before it was quite dark, the old man also went to bed, for he got up at sunrise, which came very early in summer on the mountain. During the night the wind blew so hard that the whole hut shook, and all the beams creaked. The wind roared and moaned in the big chimney; and in the old pine tree it broke some branches off as if in anger.

It awakened the old man and he rose, thinking, "The little one will be afraid."

He climbed the ladder, and went softly into Heidi's loft. The moon was shining brightly through the round hole in the roof, and the beams fell on Heidi's bed. The child slept peacefully, her cheeks rosy, one round arm under her head. Her little face beamed with contentment. Grandfather stood long, gazing at the sleeping child, until clouds obscured the moon. Then he turned and went down the ladder.

Chapter 3

IN THE PASTURE

HEIDI was awakened early on the following morning by a loud whistle. A yellow sunbeam, shining through the opening in the loft fell on her bed, turning it, and all the hay that was spread about, to gleaming gold. She looked about her, astonished, not sure of where she was.

Then she heard her grandfather's deep voice, and remembered everything: how she came to the Alm yesterday, and now lived with her grandfather, and no longer with the old Ursel. Besides being quite deaf, old Ursel was always so chilly that she was forever sitting by the kitchen fire or by the stove, where Heidi had to sit also, or be quite near, so the old woman might see what she was doing, as she could not hear. Poor Heidi had always felt stifled in that room. How glad she was now to awaken in her new home, to recall how much she had seen on the mountain the day before, and to think of all the new things in store for her today and above all Schwänli and Bärli!

Jumping up from her bed, she put on all the clothes of the day before – and they were few enough! She clambered down and ran out of doors. There stood Peter, the goatherd with his flock, and Grandfather was bringing out his goats from the shed to join the others. Heidi ran from one to another to say good morning.

"Would you like to go to the pasture?" Grandfather asked.

"Oh, yes!" Heidi replied jumping for joy.

He smiled. "You must wash first, however, and make yourself clean. See, everything is ready for you." He pointed to a large tub of water that stood warming in the sun before the door. Heidi plunged her arms in and splashed and rubbed herself until her skin shone. Grandfather, in the meanwhile, went into the hut, and soon called Peter.

"Come here, goat-general! Bring in your knapsack, too."

Surprised, Peter obeyed and opened the bag to show his scanty dinner.

"Wider," directed the old man, and put in a large piece of bread and a generous piece of cheese. Peter's eyes opened wide, for each of the pieces was twice the size of his own.

"Now the mug for Heidi goes in, too," the old man said, "for she can't drink as you do right from the goats themselves. Milk this full twice at noon, for the child is to go with you, and stay until you return in the evening. Take care that she does not fall off the cliffs."

"Yes, Uncle," Peter nodded solemnly. "I will look after her."

Heidi came running, fresh from her washing. She had rubbed her face, neck, and arms so vigorously with the rough towel she found near the tub, that she was as red as a lobster, as she stood there before them.

The old man laughed, "You look fine now. But in the evening, when you return, you must go into the tub like a fish. When you go about as the goats do, you get very black feet. Now, on your way."

Peter and Heidi went off merrily, climbing up the Alm. The last traces of clouds were swept from the sky, and it was now a wonderful deep blue. The mountain was covered with blue and yellow flowers. Their wide-open flower faces seemed to be laughing back at the sun, while everything shimmered and shone in the clear air.

Heidi scampered this way and that, shouting for joy. Here it was a whole field of red primroses; there the place was blue with gentians. All round, tender, yellow buttercups nodded in the sunlight. Beckoned everywhere by new and delightful sights, Heidi forgot the goats and even Peter as she gathered great handfuls of flowers and stuffed them into her apron. She intended to carry them home with her and put them in the hay in her loft, to make her room look like the flower-strewn Alm.

Poor Peter felt as if his eyes had to see everywhere. For the goats, like Heidi, ran in all directions while Peter whistled and shouted and swung his rod to bring them together again and again.

"Where are you now, Heidi?" he called out almost angrily.

"Here!" she replied from somewhere and nowhere, for Peter could not see her.

Small Heidi sat nestled on the ground behind a mound covered with sweet-smelling wild flowers which perfumed the air about them. Heidi had never breathed air so delicious. She drew in great breaths, one after the other and paid no attention to her guardian, Peter.

"Come here where I can see you," shouted Peter. "You are not to fall over the cliffs. Your grandfather has forbidden it."

"What cliffs? Where are they?" Heidi asked, not stirring from the spot.

"There. Up above. We still have a long way to climb, so come along. At the very top, an old eagle sits and screams!"

That brought Heidi out at once, with her apron full of flowers.

"Pick no more of those," said Peter. "You have picked enough. Besides, if you pick them all today, tomorrow you won't find any."

The last reason convinced Heidi, and anyway, her apron was so full that there was not room for another flower.

Now she kept pace with Peter; and the goats too, went in better order, for they smelled the sweet herbs in their pasture on the heights and pushed forward steadily.

The pasture where Peter usually spent the day, was at the foot of the peak. The base, covered with scrub pines and bushes, rose steeply towards the sky. On one side of the Alm there were deep chasms, and the old man had been right to warn the children of that danger.

Having reached the highest point, Peter took off his knapsack and placed it carefully in a small hollow where it would be safe from the gusty mountain wind. Peter knew that wind very well, and he did not mean to see his knapsack and his dinner go rolling down the hillside. After making sure of its safety, Peter stretched himself on the sunny ground, to rest after the steep climb.

Observing Peter's actions, Heidi had tucked her apron into the same hollow, rolling it up first with all the flowers in it. Then she plumped herself down beside Peter, and gazed about her. Below was the valley bathed in the full glow of the morning sun. Before her, a broad white snow field rose towards the deep-blue heaven. On the left, a tremendous mass of rocks was heaped up and on each side of it rose a pillar of rock, bare and jagged against the blue sky. The great pinnacles seemed to be looking down on Heidi, so she sat subdued, and looked and looked at everything. How still it was, with only a soft breeze stirring the blue harebells, and the yellow buttercups that grew all about nodding to her from their slender stalks. She saw that Peter had gone to sleep, and the goats climbed here and there, up among the bushes.

Never had Heidi been so happy in her entire life. She drank in the sunlight, and the fragrant air, and longed to stay where she was forever.

A long, long time passed, with Heidi gazing at the rocks overhead so steadfastly that they seemed to have acquired faces, and to be watching her like old friends. All at once she heard a loud sharp scream above her. As she looked up, a huge bird, such as she had never seen before, flew in circles. With wide-spread wings it soared through the air, and then in great sweeps it came back again and again, screaming piercingly over Heidi's head.

"Peter, Peter! wake up!" Heidi cried loudly. "The great eagle is here! Look! Look!"

Peter wakened at her cry and jumped to his feet. Then both children gazed at the bird, which rose higher and higher, and finally disappeared in the blue sky over the grey rocks.

"Where has he gone?" Heidi asked breathlessly.

"To his nest, way up there."

"How beautiful to live up there!" Heidi sighed. "But why does he scream so?"

"It is the way of eagles. He can't help it."

"Let us climb up there, too. I want to see his home," Heidi begged.

"Oh, oh, oh!" cried Peter, each "oh" being louder than the last. "Even the goats cannot climb up there. And Alm-Uncle said you must not fall off the cliffs."

Suddenly Peter began to whistle and to call so loudly that Heidi did not know what was happening. But the goats knew, and all came running and leaping, and were soon gathered on the green pasture. Some nibbled at the grass, others ran about, and a pair stood opposite each other and butted playfully with their horns.

Heidi ran in among the gambolling goats, and dashed from one to another to make herself acquainted with each separately. Each had its own charm for her; each one looked and behaved differently.

While Heidi played with the goats, Peter brought out the knapsack, and arranged the food in a square on the grass. The large pieces of bread and cheese he put on Heidi's side, the small ones on his own. Then, filling the mug with fresh milk from Schwänli, he placed it in the centre of the square.

With his grass table set, Peter called Heidi, but the child was so absorbed in the pranks of her new playfellows, that she heard nothing. Now Peter shouted so loud, that he could have been heard on the topmost rocks, and this time Heidi ran to him as fast as she could. Seeing the inviting table, she hopped about it and clapped her hands.

"Stop jumping about and eat," said Peter crossly, seating himself.

"Is the milk for me?" Heidi asked.

"Yes, and the big chunks of bread and cheese are yours also. When you finish the milk, you may have another mug full from Schwänli. After you finish yours, it will be my turn."

"Where do you get your milk?" the little girl asked curiously.

"From my goat, Snail. Eat now. Go ahead."

Heidi began with the milk, and when she had emptied the mug, Peter rose and filled it again. She broke some of her bread into the milk, and then held out the rest of it towards Peter. It was a big piece, still twice as large as his, which he had already eaten, together with his cheese. Heidi looked at her cheese and then gave it to him also, the whole big lump, saying, "Take it, I've had enough."

Peter stared at Heidi, speechless. Never in his whole life had he been able to give such food away. He hesitated, for he could not believe that Heidi was in earnest, but the child smiled and nodded and at last laid the food on his knee.

Convinced that she was serious, he took the gift. While he feasted, Heidi watched the flock.

"What are the goats' names?" she asked Peter.

He knew them all, of course, and rattled the names off without hesitation, pointing each one out as he spoke. Heidi gave him her entire attention, and soon could name them all herself.

There was big Turk with powerful horns, who always

23

butted the others, so that they scampered away whenever he drew near them. They would have nothing to do with this roughneck. Only the brave, slender Thistlebird did not run away, but struck out sharply, once, twice, six times, until the great Turk stood still in astonishment and made no further trouble. Thistlebird had sharp horns, too, and knew how to use them.

Little white Snowball, who always bleated beseechingly, often had Heidi running to take its head between her hands, to comfort it. Now the child ran to it again, for she heard the wailing cry, and she put her arm around the small creature's neck saying, "What is wrong, Snowball? Why do you cry like this?"

The animal pressed close to the little girl, and was quiet.

Peter explained Snowball's trouble. "She cries because her old one does not come with us any more. She was sold to Mayenfeld, day before yesterday, and will not come to the Alm any more."

"Who is the old one?" Heidi asked.

"Its mother," Peter answered.

"Where is the grandmother?" Heidi wanted to know.

"She has none." Peter shrugged.

"And the grandfather?"

"None."

"Oh. Poor little Snowball!" Heidi moaned tenderly, pressing the goat close to her side. "Don't cry so any more. I'll come here every day, then you won't be lonely. And if you feel very badly, you may come to me."

Snowball rubbed her head against Heidi and bleated no more.

When Peter finished his ample dinner, he rose to look after his flock again. The goats had already begun to wander.

The loveliest and cleanest of the goats were Schwänli and Bärli. They behaved better than the others, and usually went their own way. They avoided Turk particularly.

The animals had begun to climb up again towards the bushes, springing lightly over every obstacle. Turk trying to give someone a blow whenever he could. Schwänli and Bärli climbed prettily, in a delicate and dainty manner. Heidi put her hands behind her back, and watched them as they went higher and higher.

Peter had thrown himself down on the ground again, and turning to him, Heidi remarked, "The prettiest of all are Schwänli and Bärli."

"Of course," Peter replied. "The Alm-Uncle brushes and combs them and gives them salt daily along with nice clean stalls."

All at once the lad sprang to his feet and was off after the goats with great leaps, and instantly Heidi was after him, for surely something must have happened, and she could not stay behind.

Peter raced through the flock towards the side of the Alm, where the rocks rose up steep and bare, and where a careless goat might easily fall, and get all its legs broken. He had noticed that the bold Thistlebird had strayed in that direction, and came after her barely in time, for she had reached the very edge of a precipice. He was about to seize her, when he tripped and fell, grasping her only by the leg as he came down hard on the ground. He didn't let go, but held her fast, though she bleated with surprise and annoyance.

The goatherd called loudly to Heidi, for he was unable to get to his feet and it seemed to him that he was pulling the little goat's leg off, she was so determined to go on. He had scarcely got her name out, when Heidi was there, beside him.

Seeing the danger of the situation, she pulled up a sweet-smelling herb and thrust it under Thistlebird's nose, soothing the creature with "Come, little goat, be good, Thistlebird. See now, you might have fallen and broken your bones and that would have hurt you, indeed."

The goat turned to nibble at the herb held out by Heidi.

Peter scrambled to his feet, and hurriedly seized the rope that hung from Thistlebird's collar, while Heidi grabbed the collar from the other side. Together they led her between them to the rest of the flock, peacefully grazing below.

With his goat safe once more, Peter raised his rod and was about to whip her soundly. Thistlebird drew back, alarmed, for she saw what was coming.

Heidi saw it, too, and screamed out in terror, "No, Peter, no! Don't hit her! See how frightened she is!"

"She deserves to be punished," Peter said angrily, and raised the rod again; but the child seized his arm, and held it.

"You must let her alone!" she cried.

Peter stared amazed by her commanding tone and flashing eyes. His arm dropped to his side. "Very well, she may go, but you will have to give me some of your cheese tomorrow." He felt that he must have some reward for the fright the silly goat had given him.

"You shall have it all, tomorrow and every day. I do not want it," said Heidi. "You may have a big piece of bread also, as big as I gave you today. But you must promise me not to hit Thistlebird or Snowball, or any of the goats."

Peter shrugged. "It's all the same to me," he said, and for him that was a promise. He let the culprit go, and the happy goat leaped back in amongst the others.

So the day had passed and now the sun began to sink behind the mountain. Heidi sat on the ground, admiring the harebells and bluebells, as they took on the glow of the golden light. The grass, too, turned a golden hue, and the rocks above seemed to shimmer and flash.

Suddenly Heidi leaped to her feet, shouting, "Peter, it's burning, it's on fire! All the mountains are aflame. Even the great snow there, and the sky. Look, the highest peak is glowing! And now it has reached the eagle's nest. The rock! the pines! everything burns!" Heidi cried.

"It is always like that," Peter said kindly, "but it is no fire."

"What then?" asked Heidi, unable to contain her excitement. "What is it, Peter?"

"It comes by itself," the lad explained.

"Oh, look, look!" Heidi screamed wildly. "It is all like red roses now – the snow and those great, pointed rocks! What are they called, Peter?"

"They don't have names," Peter answered.

"How lovely, all that rosy snow! and all over the rocks it looks like roses. Now they are turning grey! It's going! It's all gone . . . oh, Peter!" Heidi threw herself on the ground, looking as unhappy as if all the beauty in the world were coming to an end.

"It will be just so again tomorrow," comforted the lad. "Get up, we must be on our way home now." Whistling his herd together, Peter set out on the homeward journey.

"Will it be like that every single day? Always, when we go up to the pasture?" Heidi asked, longing for reassurance.

"Most always," he said.

"But surely tomorrow?"

"Of course, tomorrow."

The promise quieted the girl, and, filled with so many new impressions, she scarcely spoke a word until the Alm-hut came in view, and she saw her grandfather sitting on his bench outside, waiting for them.

Heidi ran to him, with Schwänli and Bärli at her heels.

"Come with us tomorrow! Good night," Peter called out, anxious to have Heidi's company again.

The little girl ran back to him, gave him her hand, and promised to go tomorrow. Then she said good-bye to the departing goats, throwing her arms about the neck of little Snowball. "Good night, dear Snowball. Sleep well, and don't forget that I am going with you again tomorrow, and you must not be so sad any more."

Then Heidi left her and turned back to her grandfather.

"It was so beautiful! The fire, and the roses, the blue and yellow flowers. See what I have brought you."

She opened her apron and shook out all the flowers. But what had happened? The flowers looked so different. They were like hay, and not one was open.

"What is it, Grandfather?" she cried, frightened. "They did not look like that when I picked them."

"They like to be out in the sun, not shut up in your apron," the old man told her.

"Then I'll not bring any more home. Tell me, why did the eagle scream so?" she asked anxiously, remembering the great bird.

"First you must wash, while I go to the goats' shed for the milk. Afterwards we will have supper in the house and then I'll answer all your questions."

Heidi obeyed; but later, when she sat on her new stool, and ate her bread and milk, the questions began again. "Why did the eagle scream and squawk so loudly?" she asked.

"He mocks the people who huddle together in the villages down below and corrupt one another. So he screeches at them. If they would live apart, each going his own way, up a mountain, as I have done, it would be much better, he tells them." Heidi's grandfather said this in so wild a way, the child was reminded of the screaming eagle.

"Why don't the mountains have names?" she asked.

"But they have names," he said. "Describe one to me so that I can recognize it and I will tell you what it is called."

Heidi described the great heap of rocks with the two pinnacles on each side, exactly as she had seen it.

Her grandfather looked pleased: "That one I know. It's called Falkniss. What are the others?"

"Another had a big snow field," Heidi said thoughtfully. "It looked as if it was on fire, and then it grew pink, and quite suddenly it became grey."

"I know that one," said he. "That's the Cäsaplana. I take it you liked it up there on the pastures?"

28

"Oh, yes!" Heidi told him all that had happened during the day; how beautiful it was, particularly at sunset, when everything seemed to catch fire. She begged her grandfather to explain to to her.

Grandfather stroked his beard and nodded. "Yes, the sun does that when he says good night to the mountains. He sends his most beautiful beams down upon them, so that they will know that he will come again in the morning."

The fancy pleased the child, and she could scarcely wait until the next day. But first she must sleep; and so she did in her comfortable, hay bed, and dreamed of pink mountains covered with roses, in the midst of which Snowball gambolled about merrily.

Chapter 4

THE GRANDMOTHER

NEXT morning the bright sun came again, and so did Peter with the goats, and they all climbed up to the pasture. Day after day they did this, and little Heidi became strong and brown, with never a moment of sickness. She was as merry as the birds in the trees in the green, green woods, and as happy as could be.

When autumn came, the wind blew harder over the mountains, and sometimes Grandfather would say, "You had better stay home today, Heidi. A little thing like you might be blown right down into the valley with one strong gust."

Whenever this happened, it made Peter sad. Without Heidi to keep him company, he was so lonely that he did not know what to do. Besides, when she did not come he missed his fine dinner, and the goats were now so unruly when the child was not with them, that they gave him twice as much trouble. They had become so accustomed to her that they would not go along properly without her, and ran about helter-skelter on all sides.

Heidi, however, was never unhappy. For her something interesting or amusing was always going on. But best of all she liked to go with the herd and Peter to the pasture. For there were the flowers and the eagle, and always exciting happenings with the different goats. On the other hand, in her grandfather's hut there was always hammering and sawing that was quite delightful to watch also.

But Heidi's greatest pleasure came on the day when the wind rushed and roared in the big pines behind the hut. Then she was always running out to listen to it, leaving whatever she might be doing to hear the wonderful mysterious sounds in the high branches.

The sun was now no longer warm as in the summertime, and Heidi was glad to get out her shoes and stockings, and her little coat, for every day grew colder and colder. Now, when she stood under the trees, the wind blew her about as if she were no more than a leaf. But that did not keep her from scampering out once she heard the call of the wind.

It became so cold that Peter blew upon his fingers when he came for the goats. Finally, he did not come at all, for one night a deep snow fell, and in the morning the whole Alm was white. There was not a green leaf to be seen anywhere.

Heidi sat looking through the tiny window in the hut, for it was snowing again. The thick flakes swirled through the air, and the snow piled up to the edge of the window, and then higher still, so that it could not be opened. The child and her grandfather were completely snowed in.

This, too, Heidi found enchanting. She ran about from window to window, wondering if the whole hut would be completely covered. Then they would need to have a lamp in the daytime.

But it did not get to be as bad as all that. The snow ceased on the following day, and the old man went out to shovel a path all around the house, piling the snow in great heaps.

Now the windows were free, and the door too, which was a good thing, for as Heidi and her grandfather sat down to dinner together, there suddenly came a great knocking and kicking at it. When the door opened, there stood Peter. But he had not kicked and stamped so rudely without reason. It was to clear his shoes of the clinging snow. In fact, the whole of Peter was like a snowman, for he had forced his way through the drifts, and frozen snow clung to him all over. Nothing had turned him back, however, for he wanted to see Heidi. A week was too long for him to be away from her.

"Good evening," he said and moved as near the fire as possible.

He did not say another word, but his whole face beamed, because he was happy to be there. Heidi stared at him and marvelled, for now that he was near the fire, the snow began to melt and he looked like a waterfall.

Grandfather nodded to him. "Ah, General, and how are you getting on these days? Now that your army is disbanded you must chew on your slate-pencil, I suppose."

Heidi was instantly alert. "Why must he chew on his slate-pencil?" she asked.

"He has to go to school in the wintertime," explained her grandfather. "There one must learn to read and write, and that is difficult. Sometimes it helps to bite the slate-pencil. Hey, General?"

"It does," said Peter.

Heidi's interest was fully caught now and she began to ask such a great number of questions about the school, that the time flew. While Peter answered her, he became quite dry from top to toe.

Peter was no great talker and it was an effort for him to explain himself clearly. This time it was especially difficult, for he no sooner explained one thing than Heidi had two or three more questions ready, and they could never be answered with a plain yes or no.

The old man listened silently, but the corners of his mouth often twitched with amusement.

At last he said, "Come, General, you have been under fire long enough and need some nourishment," and rising, he went to the cupboard to get Peter's supper, while Heidi bustled about setting the table.

Now that the old man no longer lived alone, he had made all sorts of seats for two people, including a long bench, which Heidi dragged up to the table.

They all sat comfortably, and Peter's round eyes opened wide at the sight of the huge piece of dried meat the Alm-Uncle set before him on a thick slice of bread.

The lad enjoyed himself so much he did not want to think of going home again. And yet he must, for it was growing dark.

Reluctantly he said good night, and God bless you, and was already in the doorway, when he turned back to add, "I shall come again next Sunday, a week from today. And you must come to see my grandmother, sometime. She said so."

The idea of such a visit took root in Heidi's mind at once. On the very next day she said, "Grandfather, I must go to Peter's grandmother. He did say she expects me."

"There is too much snow," he objected, putting her off.

But the project remained uppermost in the child's mind. Scarcely a day passed that she did not mention at least five or six times, "Grandfather, I really must go, surely, for Peter's grandmother expects me."

On the fourth day everything snapped and cracked from the cold. The snow was frozen hard, and yet the sun shone brightly through the window as Heidi sat on her high stool at dinner.

She began on her little speech at once. "Today certainly I must go to Peter's grandmother, or she will grow tired of waiting for me."

Grandfather looked at her steadily, then he rose from the table, and climbed up into the loft. When he came down again, he brought with him the thick sack that had served Heidi for a coverlet. "Put on your coat and come along," he said.

Heidi needed no second invitation. She ran out after him, into the glittering world of snow.

Grandfather went into the shed and then reappeared, carrying a large sledge. It had a bar across the front, and from the low seat one could steer it in any direction. The old man seated himself on the sledge, and taking Heidi in his lap, wrapped her snugly in the sack. Holding her tightly with his left arm he seized a pole with his right hand, gave a tremendous shove with his feet, and away went the sled straight down the Alm, so fast that Heidi thought they were flying, and shouted with joy.

The sledge stopped, all at once, directly in front of goat-Peter's door. Grandfather took Heidi's wraps off and set her on the ground, bidding her to go in. But she was to come out as soon it began to grow dark, and start for home. Then he turned the sled around and began the climb back up the mountain.

Heidi opened the door, and entered a little dark room. It was the kitchen, for she could see a hearth, and plates and dishes on the shelves. She went through another door and came into another small narrow room. Peter's house was not a mountain cottage like the Alm-Uncle's, which had only one large room, with a hayloft above. This one was a very old little dwelling, and everything was narrow, small, and not very comfortable looking, Heidi thought.

When she stepped into this room, Heidi found herself in front of a table at which a woman sat mending trousers. They were Peter's. Heidi recognized them immediately.

In the corner Heidi saw a bent little old woman, at a spinning wheel. She knew at once who that was, and went straight to her.

"Good day, Grandmother," she said politely. "At last I

33

have come to see you. Did you think I took too long about it?"

The grandmother raised her head and reached out to find Heidi's small hand. After she had held it in her own for a while, she said, "Are you the child who lives up with the Alm-Uncle? Are you Heidi?"

"Yes, I'm Heidi, and I've just come down the mountain with my grandfather on a big sled."

"Is that so, indeed! And yet you have such nice warm hands. Brigitte, tell me, did the Alm-Uncle, himself, come down with the child?"

Peter's mother, Brigitte, put down her mending and came to look at the child curiously, inspecting her from head to foot.

"I don't know, Mother, whether Alm-Uncle, himself, came with her," she said slowly. "It's not likely."

Heidi gazed fixedly at the woman. "I know very well who wrapped me in the coverlet from my bed and brought me down on the sled in his arms. It certainly was my grandfather."

"It must be true then what Peter has been telling us all summer," the old woman murmured. "Who would have believed such a thing! I did not think a child could live three weeks up there. How does she look, Brigitte? Tell me."

"She is delicately built, as Adelheid, her mother was. But she has black eyes and curling hair, like Tobias, and old Alm-Uncle up there. Really, she looks like both of them."

While the woman talked over her head, Heidi had looked about and noted everything in the room. Now she said, "See that shutter, Grandmother, it's swinging to and fro in the wind. My grandfather would drive a nail into it at once to hold it fast. Otherwise it will soon break one of the panes. Look, how it bangs about!"

"Dear child," the old woman said, "I cannot see it, but I can hear it only too well, and much more besides the shutter. Everything creaks and cracks in this house when the wind blows. And the wind itself comes in, too. Nothing holds together here. Sometimes, in the night, when the others are asleep, I am often afraid that the house will fall in upon us. There is no one to do anything to the house and young Peter understands nothing at all."

"But why can't you see the shutter, Grandmother? Look, it is right there!" Heidi pointed it out carefully with her finger.

"Child, child, I can see nothing," the grandmother said sadly.

"If I go out and open the shutter wide and let all the light into the room, won't you be able to see then, Grandmother?"

"No, not even then. Nobody can make it light for me any more."

"But if you go out into the bright snow, surely it is bright for you, then. Come with me, Grandmother, I'll show it to you!" Heidi took the old hand to draw her out, for suddenly she began to be terribly afraid that it could never be light again for her, either.

"No. Let me be, you good child. It will always remain dark for me, no matter if it's snow or sunshine."

"Even in summer," Heidi began, searching more and more anxiously for some comfort. "In summer, when the sun gets hot, and then says good night to the mountains, until they glow as if they were on fire, then it will be light again for you."

"Ah, child," the old woman shook her head. "It will never be light for me in this world. Never again."

At this, Heidi burst into floods of tears and loud sobs. "Who can make it light for you again? Can anybody? Is there nobody who can?"

Now the grandmother had to comfort the child, but it was not easy. Heidi seldom cried, but when she once started, it was almost impossible for her to stop. Although the grandmother tried everything she could think of to distract Heidi from her grief, it was to no avail. It pained the old woman to hear the child sobbing so, as if her heart would break.

At last she said, "Come here, dear Heidi, and I will tell you something. When one can't see, then listening can be most pleasant. Come, sit by me, and talk to me. Tell me what you do way up there on the Alm. Tell me what your grandfather does. Long ago I used to know him, but I have heard nothing about him for many years now except what Peter tells me – and that is not too much."

Heidi wiped away her tears and said consolingly: "Just wait a bit, Grandmother, and I will tell my grandfather all about you. He can surely make it light for you again. And he can mend your cottage so it will not fall to pieces. He can make everything right."

The old woman smiled gently but said nothing. Heidi began to tell her about her life up on the mountain, and about the days spent in the pasture, and the winter life indoors. She told how her grandfather could make anything out of wood – three-legged stools, benches and chairs and mangers into which hay could be put for Schwänli and Bärli. He had just finished a big new tub for summer bathing, and a new porringer and some spoons. Heidi became quite excited as she recounted the wonderful things his skilful hands fashioned from the wood.

The old lady listened to all this with great interest, calling out to Brigitte now and then, "Do you hear what the child tells me about the Alm-Uncle? Is it not remarkable?"

Suddenly there was a great stamping at the door and Peter burst into the room. He stood stock still with his big round eyes and mouth open when he saw Heidi and she cried, "Good evening, Peter."

"Are you out of school already, Peterkin?" the grandmother said. "The afternoon has not passed so quickly for me for many a year. How is the reading going?"

"About the same," Peter replied, making a face.

"Well now, I thought there might be a little change by

this time. Remember! You will be twelve years old come February," the old woman reminded him, sighing a little.

"Why should there be a change then?" asked Heidi, curiously.

"I thought perhaps he might have learned to read a little," the grandmother said wistfully, "I have an old prayer book on the shelf full of beautiful hymns. I haven't heard them for a long time, and I can't remember them any more. I hoped when Peterkin had learned to read, he would sometimes read me a hymn. But it is no use. He can't learn. It is too hard for him."

"I think I'd better light the lamp," said Brigitte, who had been working all this time at her mending. "The afternoon has flown away without my knowing it, and now it's quite dark."

"Oh!" Heidi sprang from her chair and stretched out her hand to the old lady, saying, "Good night, Grandmother, I must go straight home now." She shook hands with Peter's mother, and hurried towards the door.

"Wait, child, wait!" cried the grandmother anxiously. "You cannot go alone. Peterkin must go with you. Take care of the child, Peter, and do not let her stand still, lest she be frostbitten. Has she a warm shawl?"

"I haven't any shawl, but my coat is warm. I shan't be cold," Heidi assured her and she was out of the house in an instant, running so nimbly that Peter could not overtake her for a while.

The children had not gone far up the mountain when they saw the Alm-Uncle coming towards them. In a few great strides he was beside them.

His white head nodded as he looked down at Heidi. "You have kept your promise," he said, "that is good," and wrapping her carefully again in the coverlet, he took her in his arms and turned back towards his hut.

Brigitte, who had run out of the house to watch the children, went back in with Peter, to tell her mother what they had seen.

The old woman threw up her hands in surprise. "Thank God that the Alm-Uncle is so kind to Heidi! I hope he will permit the little one to come to me again. It has done me a world of good. What a kind heart she has, and how she can talk!"

Even when the grandmother went to bed, she kept talking about Heidi. "If only she would come again! I would have something to look forward to. She is such a dear and happy child."

Brigitte agreed heartily with this, and Peter grinned and nodded vigorously.

All this time while Heidi went up the mountain in her grandfather's arms, she chattered without ceasing, but as nothing could get through the coverlet so closely wrapped about her, Alm-Uncle could not understand a single word. "Wait a bit," he said at last. "Wait until we reach home, child. Then you can tell me everything."

So just as soon as they reached the hut, and Heidi was free of her warm wrappings, she began, "Tomorrow we must take your hammer and the nails and go down to Peter's house, Grandfather. The shutters shake so. We must make them fast, and make everything else fast, too, for the whole place creaks and rattles dreadfully."

"Must we, indeed? Who says we must?" demanded the old man.

"I do," Heidi replied stoutly. "Everything is so loose there, that it makes the grandmother so afraid. Sometimes she cannot sleep because she fears the house will fall to pieces on top of them all. And oh, Grandfather, she says that no one can make it light for her again, but surely you can! Think how sad it must be for her always to sit in the dark. Tomorrow we will help her, won't we?"

The old man looked at her for a long time in silence, then he said, "Yes, Heidi, tomorrow we will make things fast for the grandmother, just as you say."

Heidi threw her small arms around the old man, shouting, "Tomorrow we will go! Tomorrow we will go!"

The old man was as good as his word, and the following afternoon the two rode the sled down the Alm as before. Again he set the child on the ground before the cottage door, saying, "Go in now, but when it is evening, come out." Then laying the sack-coverlet on the sled, he went round about the cottage.

Scarcely had Heidi opened the door and stepped into the room, when the grandmother called out from her corner. "The child is here again! Heidi has come back!" She stopped the spinning wheel and stretched out her arms to embrace her small friend.

Heidi pushed a stool close to the old woman and had just seated herself when suddenly there came such a pounding and banging on the outside of the cottage that the grandmother started and almost overturned her spinning wheel in her fright. "It has come!" she cried. "It has come! The cottage is falling down!"

But Heidi took hold of her hands and said soothingly, "No, no, Grandmother, don't be afraid! It is only my grandfather with his hammer making things fast about your house so that you need not be uneasy any more."

"Is that true? Can it be possible? Then the good Lord has not forgotten us!" the old woman cried. "Go out, Brigitte, and if it is the Alm-Uncle ask him to come in for a moment. I want to thank him."

Brigitte obeyed, going up to him saying, "Good day, Uncle, and my mother greets you also. No one has ever done us such a kindness before and my mother wishes to thank you in there," she gestured to the doorway of the house.

"Enough!" the old man interrupted. "I know very well what you think of the Alm-Uncle. Go on back into the house. Whatever else needs to be done here I can find out for myself."

Brigitte went from him immediately. One never argued with Alm-Uncle.

Left alone he pounded and hammered on all sides of the

rickety cottage. Then he climbed to the roof, hammering here and there until he had used up all the nails he had brought with him. By the time he was finished it was quite dark. Just as he came down to fetch his sledge, Heidi stepped out of the door.

Grandfather wrapped her up and took her on one arm, and dragging the sledge behind him, up he went to their hut.

And so the winter passed. Heidi had come into the joyless life of the blind woman, bringing happiness with her. The old grandmother's days were no longer dark, one just like the other. Every morning she listened for the light footsteps she loved so well, and when Heidi danced in, she called out joyfully to the child.

Seated on her little stool near the grandmother, Heidi chattered about all sorts of pleasant things. The old woman felt so happy that the hours flew by.

Heidi had become deeply attached to the grandmother, and when she remembered the old lady's blindness which no one, not even her grandfather, could help to overcome, her heart was so sad. But the grandmother's constant assurance that she scarcely minded her misfortune when Heidi was with her, consoled the child, and she came down to her on the sled every fine winter afternoon.

Without anything more being said, the Alm-Uncle had each time taken his hammer and other tools along and had pounded and mended and put things in shape on the outside of goat-Peter's cottage. It no longer rattled and banged and creaked the long nights through, and the grandmother slept peacefully, often declaring that she would never cease to be grateful to the Alm-Uncle.

Chapter 5

A VISIT, AND ANOTHER,
AND THE CONSEQUENCES

THE winter quickly passed and still more quickly another enchanting summer, then another winter came to its end. Heidi was as happy as the birds in the sky, looking forward to the coming of spring, when the south wind would again blow through the pines and sweep away the snow. Soon the bright sun would bring out the blue and yellow flowers, and then the days for the pasture would come. Those were the most beautiful days that could be imagined for Heidi. She was now eight years old, and had learned all manner of useful things from her grandfather. She took care of the goats, and Schwänli and Bärli ran after her like faithful dogs, bleating for joy when they so much as heard her voice.

Twice during the winter Peter had brought word from the schoolmaster of Dörfli to the Alm-Uncle, saying that he should send Heidi to school; she was more than old enough. Indeed she should have gone the winter before. Each time the old man answered that if the schoolmaster had anything to say to him, he could always be found on the Alm. Actually, there was no thought in his mind of sending Heidi to school.

When the March sun began to melt the snow, and the white snowdrops peeped out in the valley, and on the Alm the pines waved their boughs merrily in the wind once more, Heidi ran again and again into the hut to tell her grandfather how much larger the strip of green had become under the trees. She could hardly wait for summer to cover the mountain with grass and flowers.

One sunny morning, as Heidi was bounding outdoors,

she almost fell backwards into the hut from fright, for before her stood an old man, dressed in black. He gazed at her earnestly, and seeing her fear, said in a kindly tone, "Do not be afraid of me. I love children very much. Give me your hand, for you must be Heidi, and tell me, where is your grandfather?"

"He is in here cutting round spoons out of wood," Heidi told him, and opened the door wider.

This was the good pastor from Dorfli, who had known the Uncle long ago when he lived in the valley and they had been neighbours. He now stepped into the hut and went over to the old man, who was bent over his work. "Good morning, neighbour!" he said softly.

Grandfather looked up in surprise, and then, rising, said, "Good morning, Pastor!" and at once offered his own chair to the guest.

"It has been a long time since I've seen you, neighbour," the pastor said.

"Yes. It has been a long time," the Alm-Uncle agreed.

"I have come here today to speak to you about something of importance," began the pastor. "I think that you have already guessed what it is."

The good man stopped and looked at Heidi, who was inspecting him with equal interest from the doorway.

"Go out to the goats, child," said her grandfather. "Take some salt with you, and stay with them until I come."

Heidi gave him a short nod and disappeared at once.

"That child should have gone to school long ago," the pastor said. "The teacher sent you word, but you have given him no answer. What do you mean to do about it?"

"I mean not to send her to school," the Alm-Uncle replied coolly. Astonished the pastor stared at the old man, who sat with folded arms upon his bench and looked unyielding.

"What are you going to do for this child then?" he asked.

"Nothing. She grows and she thrives with the goats and

the birds. With them she learns no evil. She is safe from harm."

"But she is neither a goat, nor is she a bird. Heidi is a human child. If she learns nothing evil from such company, she learns, on the other hand, nothing else. But she should learn; and it is high time, too, that she began her schooling. I have come to warn you, neighbour, so that you can be thinking about this and make your plans during the summer. This must be the last season that the child runs about wild, without proper instruction. Next winter she must go to school, and go every day."

The old man shook his head, unmoved.

"Is there no way to bring you to your senses? How can you be so stubborn?" asked the pastor, getting quite out of patience with the Alm-Uncle. "You have travelled about the world a great deal, and must have learned much. Surely you have more wisdom than you're showing, neighbour."

"Indeed!" replied the old man, and his voice, too, showed that he was losing patience, "and does the pastor think that it really would be wise for me to send a tender child down the mountain every day next winter? In snow and wind – a two hours' journey? And then have her coming up again every evening, when grown men can scarcely manage it? Perhaps the pastor can recall the child's mother, Adelheid. You could scarcely say she was a robust woman. Shall I endanger the health of this child through over-exertion? Let someone try to force me! I will go into court to see if I can be forced."

"On that score you are right, neighbour," replied the pastor, his tone more gentle. "The little one could not be sent to school from here. I can see that you love her dearly. Therefore, do something for her sake that you should have done long before. Come down into Dorfli, and live again amongst your fellow men. What kind of life can it be that you lead up here, bitter with God and man? Besides, should anything happen to you here during the winter, how could help reach you? I cannot understand how you can manage

43

to get through the winter, and with this child, too, without freezing."

"The child has young blood, warm clothing, and snug shelter. Moreover, I know where to get wood, and the best time to fetch it. My shed is amply stocked, and in my hearth the fire never goes out the winter long. Down there the people despise me, and I them. It's best, then, that we remain apart."

"No, no, this life up here is not good for you! I know your trouble," said the pastor earnestly. "As for the village folk not liking you, what does that matter? Seek to make your peace with God, ask His Forgiveness if you have done any wrong and then come and see how differently people will regard you, how pleasant it will be for you to live as other men, among your fellows."

The good man rose and held out his hand to the Alm-Uncle. "I shall look forward next winter to having you again amongst us. You and I have been old friends, and I do not wish to see any force used against you. Give me your hand upon it, promise that you will come back to Dorfli, and live again at peace with God and man."

The Alm-Uncle gave his hand, but he also said quite decidedly, "I know that you mean well, Pastor, but I cannot do what you ask. I will not send the child to school, nor will I come back to Dorfli, and that is final."

"May God help you!" said the pastor shaking his head sadly, as he went out the door and down the mountain.

The pastor's visit put the old man out of humour, and later, when Heidi said, "Now shall we go to the grandmother?" he answered, "Not today," and would not speak again that whole afternoon.

Next morning, when the child said, "Today we'll go to the grandmother, won't we?" he was again very short with her, only saying, "We'll see."

But before the dinner table was cleared that evening, they had another visitor. Dete! She wore a fine hat with a curling feather, and a dress that swept up everything on the

44

floor of the mountain cottage. Alm-Uncle looked her up and down without a word.

Dete, however, made every effort to be agreeable, and began at once by saying that Heidi looked so wonderfully well that she could scarcely recognize the child. It was plain that the grandfather had cared for her well. Then she declared that she had always meant to take the child back again, for she fully understood what a trouble it must be for him to have charge of her. But, up to now she had not been able to provide for her.

Today she came, however, because she had just heard of something which might be of such advantage to Heidi that she could scarcely believe it herself. She had looked at once into the matter and now it was as good as settled, and such an extraordinary piece of luck rarely happened. Heidi was indeed fortunate.

It seemed that very rich relations of the family with whom she lived, who owned almost the handsomest house in all of Frankfurt, had an only daughter. This child was not well and was obliged to spend her days in a wheelchair, because she could not walk. The girl was much alone, and had to study alone with her teachers, which was most tiresome for her. So it was thought to find a young companion for her – a girl to live in the house and be her playmate.

When Dete had learned that what they wanted was an unspoiled little girl, unlike most children, she had at once thought of Heidi. She had gone to see the housekeeper, who had charge of the invalid and had given her such a glowing description of her little niece that the lady agreed at once she was exactly what was wanted.

One could scarcely guess, Dete continued, what might be in store for Heidi. When she once came to live with these people, she would have everything that the daughter had. And, no one could tell, the daughter was so delicate in health – if the family should be left without a child, what a wonderful piece of luck that might be for Heidi.

"Have you finished?" interrupted the grandfather, who thus far had not said a word.

"Well!" Dete cried, tossing her head. "You act as if I'd brought you an ordinary piece of news. But there is not in all Prättigau a single person who would not have thanked God on his knees for such tidings as I have just given you."

"Take them, then, where you choose. I don't want them," the old man said harshly.

At these words, Dete blew up like a skyrocket.

"Well, if that's your opinion, I will tell you what I think! This child is now eight years old, and she knows nothing, and can do nothing, and you will not let her learn in school nor in church. They told me all about it in Dorfli.

"She is my only sister's child, and I must answer for what happens to her; and when such a chance as this falls to the child's lot, there can be but one opinion on it, and what is more, there is not one single person down in Dorfli who will not help me against you. And if you wish to come before the court, you'd better think twice about it."

"Hold your tongue!" roared the old man, his eyes blazing. "Take the child, and be gone. Never bring her into my sight again. I don't want to see her with such a hat and feather on her head, and such words in her mouth as you have spoken today." And with great fierce strides he stomped out of the hut.

"You have made grandfather angry," Heidi said, her black eyes snapping.

"Oh, he'll get over it soon," Dete said. "Come now, where are your clothes, child?"

"I am not going with you," Heidi declared.

"What did you say?" Dete began dangerously, then thinking better of it, continued, in a less angry fashion. "Come, come, you don't know what you are saying. It will be far pleasanter for you there than here, believe me."

Going to the cupboard, Dete took out Heidi't things, and packed them together hastily. "Come, get your hat. It is not becoming, but it will do for the present. Put it on, and let us be off."

"But I am not going," Heidi repeated.

"Stop acting like an obstinate goat. You must have learned it from them. You heard what your grandfather said. He wants us to go, and he does not want to see us again. Don't anger him still more by lingering. You have no idea how pleasant it is in Frankfurt, nor all the things you will see there. And, if you don't like it there, you can come back here again. By that time your grandfather's temper will have cooled."

"Can I come home again this evening?"

"What? Oh, come along! Didn't I tell you that you could come back? Today we must go to Mayenfeld, then early tomorrow morning we shall take a train and in that you can come back here in a trice. It's like flying."

Aunt Dete took the child's hand firmly in hers, and with the bundle of clothes on her arm, hurried her down the mountainside.

As it was too early to take the goats to pasture, Peter was still at school in Dorfli, or rather he should have been, but he now and again played truant. "It is not of the least use for me to go to school," he thought. "I cannot learn to read, so I would do much better to go about searching for wood, which can at least be burned."

So he was on the mountainside not far from his cottage, with a bundle of sticks on his shoulder. He stared at the pair as they came down towards him, and when they were close, he said, "Where are you going?"

"I have to go to Frankfurt with Aunt Dete," Heidi explained, "But first I will run in to see the grandmother."

"No, no! There is no time for talk; it is already late!" Dete said anxiously, and held the child fast by the hand. "You can come back to see her soon, but now we must hurry." And she did not release Heidi, for fear the child might take it into her head not to go, and that the grandmother might also urge her to remain.

47

But Peter loped into the cottage and flung his bundle of sticks down with such violence that his grandmother started from her spinning and cried aloud.

"What is the matter, Peterkin? What has happened?"

And his mother, too, who had been sitting at the table, almost flew into the air as she cried, "What is it? What has made you so wild?"

"She — she has taken Heidi away!" exclaimed Peter, almost beside himself.

"Who? Who?" wailed the grandmother. But she must have guessed what had happened, for Brigitte had told her that she had seen Dete going up the mountain to the Alm-Uncle's. Trembling with haste, the old woman pushed open the window, and called out beseechingly, "Dete, Dete! Do not take Heidi away! Bring her back! Please!"

The travellers were still within earshot, but Dete only held the child faster, and increased her pace to a run.

"But the grandmother is calling me!" Heidi protested.

Dete forced the child along, lest they miss the train for Frankfurt, she said. Once there, Heidi would not want to return, but if she should, there might be some nice gift to bring to the grandmother.

This idea appealed to Heidi, and she began to run of her own accord. "Yes, yes. Let us go quickly, Aunt Dete. Perhaps we can get to Frankfurt today, so that I can come back at once with something nice for her." It was the child who urged the aunt now.

In Dorfli Dete was quite happy to have everyone see that she was being hurried along in this way by the child herself. So she called to all who would stop her, from the houses: "You see, I can't possibly stop, Heidi is in such a hurry; and we have still far to go."

"Thank heaven you are taking her away from the Alm-Uncle!" "It is a miracle the child is living! And so rosy-cheeked, too!" Remarks of this sort reached Dete from all sides, and since Heidi said nothing, the gossipers could think what they wished.

From that day on, the Alm-Uncle appeared more wicked than ever, and when he did chance to be in Dorfli he spoke to no one, and looked so forbidding that the women said to their children, "Take care and stay out of his way, or the Alm-Uncle will get you."

The old man had nothing to do with anyone in Dorfli, but went through the village, deep down into the valley, where he exchanged his goat cheese for bread and meat. When he passed through Dorfli, the people gathered together, and each one had something strange to tell about the old man – how he looked more wild than ever, and how he never exchanged a greeting with anyone. All agreed it was lucky that the child had escaped. No wonder the little one had run as if afraid that her grandfather might pursue her and bring her back to the Alm.

Only the blind grandmother defended the old man to everyone who came to her cottage to bring her stuff to spin, or to take away the yarn that she had made. To these people she always told how good and careful the Alm-Uncle had been of the child; how he had mended her cottage and made it safe. But this talk was greeted with disbelief in Dorfli. The grandmother was too old to know what had really been going on.

So the days again grew heavy for the old grandmother, and not one passed when she did not say mournfully, "How empty my days are without the little one. Oh, if I could only hear Heidi's voice once more before I die!"

Chapter 6

A NEW LIFE FOR HEIDI

In the house of Mr. Sesemann, in Frankfurt, his ailing daughter sat in the comfortable wheelchair where she spent each day. She was in the study, which adjoined the spacious dining room. All sorts of things were arranged here for her convenience, and this was the place which the family used as a living room. Here, also, the small invalid had her daily lessons.

Klara had a thin, pale face, with gentle blue eyes, fixed at this moment on the wall clock, whose hands seemed to move especially slowly today. Klara, so seldom impatient, fretted and fidgeted. "Will the time never come, Miss Rottenmeier?" she asked again and again.

Miss Rottenmeier sat very straight at a little worktable, embroidering. She wore a peculiar kind of wrap, half cape, half collar, which gave her a majestic appearance, heightened by a kind of domed cap upon her head.

She had lived in the house ever since Klara's mother had died, and, since Klara's father was away on business most of the time, she had full charge of everything in the household. The only rule Mr. Sesemann had made was that his daughter should always be consulted, and that nothing should ever be done contrary to her wishes.

As Klara complained again about the late arrival of those whom they were expecting, Dete, with Heidi's hand in hers, stood before the Sesemann house and asked John, the coachman, if it was too late to disturb Miss Rottenmeier.

"I really can't say," he replied gruffly. "Go into the hallway and ring for Sebastian, the butler."

Dete did so, and Sebastian came down the stairs at once.

"I should like to know if I may disturb Miss Rottenmeier at this hour," Dete asked again.

"I can't say. Ring for Miss Tinette. This is her bell over here." And without another word Sebastian went off about whatever was his business.

So Dete rang again, and presently Tinette appeared on the stairs, a dazzling little white cap on the top of her head, and a rather scornful expression on her face.

"What is it?" she asked from the top of the stairs.

Dete repeated her question.

Tinette vanished, but came back almost at once, saying, "You are expected."

Still holding Heidi by the hand, Dete followed Tinette into the study. She did not let her go even there, for she did not know what the child might take it into her head to do in this strange place.

Miss Rottenmeier came forward to inspect the new playmate of the daughter of the house. Obviously the sight did not please her. Heidi wore her simple woollen dress, and her old straw hat, both much the worse for wear. In turn, Heidi looked up at Miss Rottenmeier in the most innocent way.

"What is your name, child?" Miss Rottenmeier asked after she had studied the little girl searchingly for several minutes, during which Heidi had never once dropped her own gaze.

"Heidi," the child said in a clear, sweet voice.

"What? That is no Christian name. What name was given to you at your baptism?" the lady asked.

"I don't know."

"Is that a proper answer?" The housekeeper shook her head. "Is this child being simple, or impudent, Miss Dete?"

"If you will allow me to speak for her, ma'am, she is very inexperienced," Dete said, at the same time giving her niece a secret push. "She is anything but simple, nor is she impertinent. She knows nothing of that kind of thing. She means everything precisely as she says it. Today is her first

51

time in the presence of gentlefolk, and she knows little of good manners. But she is an amiable child, and willing to learn, if you will teach her and show her what to do. Her name at baptism was Adelheid; after her mother, my late sister."

"Good! Now, that is a name one can say," replied Miss Rottenmeier. "However, Miss Dete, I must say, this child strikes me as being very strange, considering her age. I informed you that the companion for Miss Klara should be the same age as she is, in order to follow her lessons, and share her interest. Miss Klara has passed her twelfth year. How old is this girl?"

"By your leave, ma'am," Dete began. "I am not sure how old she is. She is somewhat younger than twelve but not much. I cannot say precisely – perhaps she is ten, or thereabouts."

"I am eight years old. My grandather told me so," Heidi put in forthrightly.

"What! Only eight? Why, that's four years too young! What does this mean, Miss Dete? And what have you learned, child? What books have you studied?" Miss Rottenmeier sounded most put out.

"None," Heidi answered blandly.

"None? How then did you learn to read?"

"I haven't," Heidi declared, not a bit disturbed.

"Merciful heavens! you cannot read at all?" cried Miss Rottenmeier. The housekeeper paused in order to regain her composure. "Miss Dete," she said at last, "I find nothing here that accords with our agreement. How could you bring me such a creature?"

Dete, however, remained calm. "If you will pardon me, ma'am," she replied with confidence, "the child agrees exactly with what is wanted. You seek a child unlike other children. I chose this little one because older children no longer have her kind of simplicity. She seemed to me as if made to order. Now I must be going, for my mistress expects me. I will come again as soon as they can spare me, to see how the child is getting along."

Dete bobbed a curtsy and was away, out of the door and down the stairs. Miss Rottenmeier gasped, then ran after Dete, for there were many things still to discuss if the child were to remain, and she plainly saw that Dete meant to leave her with them.

Heidi stood still where she had been left by her aunt. Klara, who until now had been only an observer in her chair beckoned to Heidi. "Come to me," she said gently.

Heidi went to the wheelchair.

"Do you like to be called Heidi rather than Adelheid?"

"My name is Heidi," the child said.

"Then I shall always call you Heidi. The name suits you. I've never heard it before, and I've never seen a girl like you. Have you always had this short curly hair?"

"I think so."

"Were you happy to come to Frankfurt?"

"No. But tomorrow I am going home again, so it does not matter," said Heidi.

"You are a strange one!" exclaimed Klara. "You were sent for expressly to stay here and study with me, and now it turns out that you cannot read. It will be fun to have lessons with you, for now they will be something different. It has always been so dreadfully dull, and the mornings seem never to end. Every morning, precisely at ten, the professor comes, and the lessons begin. Until two o'clock. That is so long!

"Often the professor holds his book before his face so as to hide his yawns. And Miss Rottenmeier holds a handkerchief over her face, as if she were much amused at something we are reading. Only I know very well that she, too, is yawning behind it. And then I should like to yawn, too, but if I yawn – even once – Miss Rottenmeier will say that I am weak. And then she fetches the cod-liver oil! And I hate to take that stuff, so I swallow my yawns. But with you here, it will be so much pleasanter, for I can listen while you learn to read."

Heidi shook her head doubtfully. After all, Peter had not learned to read.

"But Heidi, you must learn to read. Everyone must. And the professor is kind. He never gets angry, and he explains everything."

At this moment Miss Rottenmeier returned. She had not been able to call Dete back, and was rather agitated. She had undertaken this business of a companion for Klara on her own responsibility, and now it did not seem likely to prove at all satisfactory. How could she get out of it? She needed time to think.

Miss Rottenmeier hurried into the dining room, past Sebastian who was setting the table, and called for Tinette with such a disagreeable voice that the lady's maid minced in with much smaller steps than she usually took. She stood before the housekeeper with so mocking a face that Miss Rottenmeier did not dare to rebuke her, but tried, instead, to control herself.

"The room for the child must be put in order," she said, with a great effort at calmness. "It needs dusting."

"For that one?" Tinette said ironically, and went away.

Sebastian now opened the folding doors between the dining-room and the study with a bang, and walked into the study, to roll Klara's wheelchair to the table. While he was working at the handle at the back, Heidi placed herself in front of him, and stared at him so fixedly, that he exclaimed, "Well what do you find so remarkable about me?" in a tone he would not have dared to use if the housekeeper had been present. But she already stood in the doorway, and heard Heidi's answer.

"With your round eyes, you look exactly like goat-Peter."

Not knowing what to make of this, Miss Rottenmeier could only clasp her hands.

Klara's chair was rolled to the table, and carefully placed

54

there. The housekeeper took the one next to her young mistress, and Heidi was directed to the one opposite.

At Heidi's plate lay a beautiful white roll. The child looked at it longingly, but sat perfectly still until Sebastian came round to her with a big dish of baked fish. Then she pointed to the roll and asked, "May I have it?"

The servant nodded, casting a side glance at Miss Rottenmeier. Heidi seized the roll and stuffed it into her pocket. Sebastian wanted to laugh, but he knew it would not be tolerated. So, keeping a straight face, he stood before Heidi, as he dared not speak, and certainly could not leave the room, until the service was completed.

Heidi stared at him, then asked, "Shall I eat some of that?"

Again Sebastian nodded.

"Then put some here," she said and looked down at her plate.

Sebastian's face took on an alarming hue, and the dish in his hand began to shake.

"You may set the tray upon the table," Miss Rottenmeier said severely, "and you may go."

The housekeeper sighed. "As for you, Adelheid, I see that I must instruct you in everything. In the first place, this is what is proper when you are at table," and a lecture, minute in every detail, followed concerning all the etiquette required while being served. "Also, you must particularly remember not to speak to him unless you have some truly necessary question to ask. Do you understand?"

Now followed a multitude of rules about getting up and going to bed, entering and leaving a room, about being orderly, and closing the doors quietly. In the middle of it all, Heidi fell asleep, for she had been up since five o'clock that morning, and had made a long journey besides. At long last Miss Rottenmeier finished her instructions with a crisp, "Now think it all over, Adelheid," she said. "Have you understood me?"

Klara could hardly keep from laughing. "Oh, Miss

Rottenmeier," she said, "Heidi has been asleep for a long time. I don't think she's heard a thing." For the invalid this remarkable dinner had been the most diverting that she'd ever known.

"Never in my life have I imagined anything like this child!" Miss Rottenmeier exclaimed angrily, and rang the bell so violently that Tinette and Sebastian came running together.

The weary child did not waken, in spite of all the commotion and had to be carried to her bedrooom, through the dining room, the study, Klara's room, and Miss Rottenmeier's, until her own corner chamber was reached.

Chapter 7

A DAY OF TROUBLES

WHEN Heidi awakened on her first day in Frankfurt, she was greatly puzzled by what she saw. She was sitting up in a high white bed in a large room. Where the light streamed in hung long white curtains. Nearby stood two chairs, decorated with great flowers. Against the wall was a sofa, with the same flowers, and before this was a round table. In the corner stood a washstand, with a number of things upon it such as Heidi had never seen before.

All at once she remembered that she was in Frankfurt, and the events of the day before rushed to her mind. Heidi jumped down from her bed and got herself dressed. Then she went to the window. She must see the sky, and the earth. It seemed to her as if she were in a cage behind the long curtains. She could not draw them aside, so she crawled under them to get to the window. But it was so high that she could just barely look out, and she did not find what she wanted. She ran from window to window but the same thing met her eyes: walls and windows, and another wall and more windows. This Heidi could not understand, and it troubled her.

It was still quite early, for Heidi was used to getting up then on the Alm, and to running out at once to see what the weather was like, and if the wind sang in the pines, and if any new flowers had blossomed. Like an imprisoned bird, she now flew from window to window, trying to open them, for she felt that she must see something besides walls and windows outside. There must be green grass on the earth, and the last traces of melting snow on the mountain and Heidi longed for the sight.

But the windows were tightly closed, and no matter how hard the child tugged, she could not force them open. She gave that up and wondered if she could not perhaps get out of the house, and run behind it until she found the grass, for she remembered that when she came here with Dete, they had passed over nothing but stones all the way. There was a knock on the door, and Tinette looked in to say, "Breakfast's ready!"

Heidi had no idea that this meant that she was to go to breakfast in the dining room. So she took a footstool from beneath the table, and taking her seat, waited patiently to see what would happen next. After a while, something did. It was a highly exercised Miss Rottenmeier, who hurried into the room. "Whatever is the matter with you, Adelheid? Don't you know what breakfast means? Come with me at once!"

This Heidi understood, of course, and followed the irate lady into the dining room, where Klara had been seated for some time. She greeted Heidi pleasantly and smiled much more than usual, for she anticipated a most interesting day ahead.

Breakfast, however, proceeded without mishaps. Heidi ate her bread and butter properly; and later, when Klara was wheeled into the library, Miss Rottenmeier told the child that she was to remain with Klara until the professor came to give her lessons.

As soon as the girls were alone, Heidi asked, "How do you look out, Klara, and see the ground from the house?"

"We open the window, of course," Klara said, amused.

"But these windows won't open," Heidi said sadly. "I've tried."

"Oh, but they will." Klara reassured her. "You can't open them, and I can't help you. But when you see Sebastian, he will open one at once if you'll just ask him."

This Heidi heard with great relief.

And now Klara began to ask Heidi about her life at home; with her eyes shining Heidi told all about the Alm, the goats, the pasture and everything that she loved up there.

Meanwhile, the professor had arrived, but Miss Rottenmeier drew him into the dining-room instead of allowing him to go to the study. There she explained the dilemma in which she now found herself and how it had all happened. How she had written to Paris to tell Mr. Sesemann that his daughter had long wished for a companion, and that she herself felt that it would help Klara in her studies and amuse her, besides. Also Miss Rottenmeier felt that it would be most agreeable to herself to be released from being constantly with her young mistress.

Mr. Sesemann had replied that he would gladly comply with his daughter's wish, but that such a playmate must be treated as if she were a daughter of the house.

Now Miss Rottenmeier said the professor must hear how unlucky she had been in her choice, and she poured out a detailed report on the ignorant, impossible Heidi. Not only must the child's education begin with the alphabet, but every point of mannerly behaviour must be taught her from the very beginning.

She saw but one way out of this unbearable position, and that was for the professor to declare that for two children who were in such different stages of advancement to study together would be most unprofitable – especially for Klara. Such a statement would then give Mr. Sesemann grounds for withdrawing from the arrangement, and the child could then be sent back to her home. But this was a step Miss Rottenmeier dared not take, now that the master of the house knew that the child had arrived.

But the professor was never one-sided in his decisions, so now he soothed Miss Rottenmeier with the prospect that if the little girl were backward on one side, she might very well be ahead in another, and some well-regulated teaching would soon bring things into proper balance.

This fair-minded attitude convinced the housekeeper that she could hope for no support from the professor, but that he intended to begin with the teaching of the alphabet.

When he had gone into the study, she strode up and down the dining-room considering her problem from every angle. She was not, however, allowed to pursue her thoughts for long, because suddenly there was a great crash in the study, followed by a frantic call for Sebastian.

Miss Rottenmeier burst into the room and stood aghast. On the floor, in the greatest confusion, lay schoolbooks, copybooks, inkstands, and on top of everything, the table-cloth, from beneath which a black stream of ink ran down the length of the room. Heidi was nowhere to be seen.

"Look at that!" cried Miss Rottenmeier, wringing her hands. "Everything ruined. I know this is the work of that wretched child."

The professor regarded the wreckage, much distressed. Klara, on the other hand, wore a rather pleased look, as she explained, "Yes, Heidi did it but it was an accident, so she must not be punished. She moved so quickly that she dragged the tablecloth with her, and so everything else fell down. Some carriages drove by, one after the other, and she rushed to see them. She has probably never seen anything like them before."

"Isn't this just as I told you, Professor?" Miss Rottenmeier said. "The creature has not the faintest idea of what lessons are nor any idea of discipline. Where is she now? If she has run away, what shall I tell Mr. Sesemann?"

Miss Rottenmeier hurried down the stairs, and there in the open doorway stood Heidi, gazing up and down the street quite puzzled.

"What are you thinking of? How dare you run off in this manner!" cried Miss Rottenmeier.

"I heard the wind in the pines, but I don't know where they are, and now I don't hear it any more," Heidi answered sadly.

What she had heard was the rumbling of heavy carriages, which seemed to her mountain-tuned ears, to be the rushing of the wind in her beloved pines. And now the sound was gone.

"Pines! Do you think we live in the forest? What an idea! Just you come upstairs with me, and see the mischief you have caused!"

Miss Rottenmeier marched upstairs, followed by Heidi, who stared at the disorder on the floor in consternation. In her joy at hearing the wind, she had thought of nothing but getting to the pines – quickly.

"Never let this happen again," said the housekeeper crossly. "In the schoolroom, one must sit still, and pay attention. If you will not do it, then, I shall tie you fast to your chair. Do you understand?"

"Yes," Heidi answered, "and I will sit still, truly."

Sebastian and Tinette came to put things to rights, and the professor went away, for there could be no lessons that day. There had certainly been no yawning that morning, either.

In the afternoon Klara had to rest for a while, and Heidi was to occupy herself as she pleased, the housekeeper explained. So when Klara was settled in her reclining chair, and Miss Rottenmeier had withdrawn to her own room, the child was free to do as she liked. And there was something she longed to do, but it was a plan for which she needed assistance. Therefore, she waited in the corridor, before the dining-room for the person to whom she wished to speak.

In a little while Sebastian came up from the kitchen with

a tray of silver to be put away in the dining-room sideboard. As he reached the top stair, Heidi confronted him, saying, "I'd like to ask you something, but it is not wrong as it was last night." She spoke very politely, for she thought he looked cross, and supposed it was on account of all that ink on the carpet.

Sebastian stared at her and laughed, for he understood at once what it all meant, and said, "Very well, Mamselle. What is it?"

"I'm not Mamselle, I'm Heidi," the child said, frowning.

"That is true, but Miss Rottenmeier has ordered me to call you Mamselle."

"Has she? Well, then, I suppose I must be," Heidi said resignedly, for she had noticed that everything in the household had to be done as Miss Rottenmeier wished.

"Now I have three names," she added, sighing.

"But what did Mamselle wish to ask?" Sebastian asked, as he went on into the dining-room.

"How does one open these windows?"

"Like this," and he opened one of the great windows easily.

Heidi ran to look out, but this window, also, was much too high.

Sebastian brought her a high wooden stool. "Now Mamselle can look out," he said, and helped her up on it.

Heidi looked, but the next moment she withdrew her head in disappointment. "There is nothing but the stone street below," she said sadly. "If you go all round the house, what is on the other side, Sebastian?"

"Nothing different," he answered.

"Isn't there any place where you can see the whole valley?" Heidi persisted.

"To do that you would have to climb up some high church tower, like that one, there, with the golden dome on the top."

Before Sebastian knew what she was about, Heidi had jumped down from her high stool and was off to the door and out into the street. But there it was not quite as she expected. The tower, seen from the window, appeared to be merely across the street. Heidi ran the whole length of the street, but could not see it anywhere. She turned a corner, going farther and farther away from the house, and still there was no tower to be seen.

Many people passed by her, but all in such haste that she thought they would not find time to answer her questions. However, on the next corner she saw a boy with a small hand organ on his back, and on the organ was a strange-looking animal, perched precariously. Running up to him, Heidi asked, "Where is the tower with the golden dome at the top?"

The boy shrugged. "I don't know."

"Who can tell me?" Heidi pleaded.

He shook his head.

"Is there any other church with a high tower?"

"Yes, there is," he said.

"Then come and show it to me."

"Tell me first what you will give me for my trouble."

The boy held out his hand. Heidi searched in her pocket, and drew out a picture of a garland of red roses. Klara had given it to her only that morning, but for a look down into the valley, to see the green grass again, she would part with it.

She held the card out to the lad. "Will you take this?"

He drew his hand back and shook his head.

"What would you like then?" she asked, tucking the picture away again.

"Money."

"I don't have any, but Klara has; she will give you some. How much do you want?"

"One mark."

"All right then, come along, show me the church."

As the boy guided her down a long street, Heidi asked what it was he carried on his back under a cloth. A beautiful organ, he told her, one that made charming music when he turned the handle. All at once he stopped and pointed to an old church with a high tower, saying, "Here it is."

Heidi saw that the door was closed. "How can I get in?" she asked.

"I don't know," the boy said.

"Do you suppose I could ring, as they do for Sebastian?"

The boy shrugged.

But Heidi had discovered a bell and now she pulled it with all her might.

"When I go up, you must wait for me down here, for I don't know my way back, and I'd want you to show me," she told the boy.

"What will you give me for my trouble?"

"Whatever you want."

"Another mark."

But the creaking lock was being turned from within and the creaking old door was being opened. An old man stepped out and stared at the children, first in surprise, then in anger.

"What do you mean by ringing my bell, you two? Can't you read the sign over the bell?   – 'For those who wish to climb the tower'. "

The lad silently pointed to Heidi, and she said at once, "That is exactly what I want to do."

"And what business have you got up there?" the old man demanded.

"I want to go up so that I can look down," Heidi told him.

"Go on home, little girl, and do not try this trick again, for I will not let you off so easily the next time!" The tower-keeper started to turn away, but Heidi held him by his coat, and begged, "Please let me go up. Only just once."

He looked around and found Heidi's eyes so beseeching that he softened, and taking the child by the hand, said kindly, "If you want to so very much, come with me."

The boy sat down on the church steps to show that he did not wish to go with them.

Heidi and the old man climbed many, many steps.

The stairway became narrower and narrower and at last it was only a small passage – and they were at the top! The tower-keeper lifted Heidi and held her at the arched window. "There! now you can look down," he said.

Heidi looked down at a sea of roofs, towers, and chimneys. She drew back, quite downcast, "It isn't anything like I expected."

"It's not, eh? And what would such a little girl know about a view? Well, let's go down, and ring no more bells at church doors," he said, putting her on the floor and leading the way back.

Where the passage widened, they came to the keeper's room. Near his door the floor extended under the sloping church roof, and there Heidi saw a big basket with a large grey cat in it. Puss was growling, for she had her family in the basket, and wanted no one to meddle with her kittens. Heidi had never seen so huge a cat, so she stopped to admire her.

Seeing the child's interest, the keeper said, "She won't hurt you while I'm here. Go and look at her kittens."

Heidi drew near the basket, and crooned with delight. "Oh the cunning little things! What beautiful kittens!" she cried again and again, enchanted by the tumbling of the seven kittens, as they rolled about in their basket.

"Would you like to have a kitten?" the keeper asked, regarding the child's joy with pleasure.

"For my very own? For always?" Heidi asked, excitedly.

"Of course. In fact, you may have them all, if you have room to keep them," said the man, happy at the prospect of getting a home for the cat family.

Heidi jumped with delight. In the big house in Frankfurt the kittens would have plenty of room. And how surprised and pleased Klara would be when she saw the dear little creatures!

"But how could I take them home with me?" Heidi asked, and reached down to take one immediately, but the big mother cat boxed her hand and spat so angrily that she drew back afraid.

"I will bring them to you, only tell me where," the old man promised, stroking the old cat to quieten her.

"To Mr. Sesemann's house," answered Heidi. "There is a golden dog's head on the door, with a thick ring in his mouth."

"I know the house well – and Sebastian, the butler, too. But to whom shall I bring the kittens? For whom should I ask? You do not belong to Mr. Sesemann, do you?"

"No. Klara does. And she will be so pleased with the kittens."

Heidi could scarcely tear herself away from the fascinations in the basket, although the keeper said it was high time to go down.

"If I could only take one or two with me! one for myself, and one for Klara! Please may I?"

"Well, perhaps it can be managed," said the keeper, and coaxing the old cat into his room, he set down a dish of milk before her. Then he shut the door upon her, and said, "Now you can take two."

Her eyes dancing, Heidi chose a white one and a yellow one striped with white, and tucked them into her pockets – one into her right-hand and the other into her left-hand – where they fitted cosily.

The organ boy was still on the steps when Heidi said goodbye to the keeper. "Which way must we take to go to Mr. Sesemann's house?" Heidi asked the lad.

"Don't know," he replied.

Heidi described the house as best she could, but the boy continued to shake his head.

"Well, look!" Heidi said, "From one of the windows you can see a big grey house with a roof that goes so," and she drew several great notches in the air with her forefinger.

The boy jumped up at this. That house he knew. He started off and soon they stood before the door with the big metal dog's head and Heidi was ringing the bell.

Sebastian appeared, and seeing Heidi, exclaimed, "Come in quickly, quickly!"

Heidi ran inside, the door slammed behind her, leaving their guide standing outside.

"Hurry, Mamselle!" urged Sebastian again. "Right into the dining-room. They are at table, and Miss Rottenmeier looks like a cannon about to burst. Whatever possessed the little Mamselle to run away?"

Heidi went into the room. Miss Rottenmeier did not look up and Klara sat silent. Sebastian pulled out Heidi's chair, and as the child took her place, the housekeeper addressed her in a solemn voice.

"Adelheid," she said, "I will speak to you later. Now I will tell you only that you have behaved shockingly, and deserve to be punished for leaving the house without asking permission, or telling anybody. And, as for running about until this late hour, it is most unheard of conduct."

"Meow!" came the surprising reply to this reprimand.

At this the housekeeper really lost her temper. "Adelheid!" she cried, "do you dare to be impertinent on top of your misbehaviour! Be careful, I warn you!"

"But I didn't," Heidi began, and was interrupted by another "Meow!"

Sebastian now almost flung his serving tray in the air and fled from the room.

"This insolence is too much!" Miss Rottenmeier croaked, for her voice was quite gone from excitement. "Leave the room," she rasped.

Although terrified, Heidi tried to explain once more. "I truly am not pert, ma'am," when again those little cat-cries came. "Meow! Meow!"

"Heidi," interposed Klara reproachfully, "when you see that it makes Miss Rottenmeier so angry, why do you persist in making that noise?"

"That's what I've been trying to tell you. I'm not. It's the kittens," Heidi burst out.

"What kittens?" screeched Miss Rottenmeier, finding her voice once more.

"Sebastian! Tinette! Find the horrid creatures. Get rid of them at once." With this she ran into the study and shut the door, for she could not bear cats or kittens.

Sebastian had to stop laughing before he could again enter the dining-room. While serving Heidi he had noticed a small kitten head, and then another, peeping out of her pockets on either side, and foresaw the trouble ahead. And it had come, as expected.

When at last he was able to re-enter the room, all seemed tranquil enough. Klara had the kittens in her lap and Heidi knelt on the floor beside her, and both girls were playing most happily with the tiny creatures.

"Sebastian," said Klara, "you must help us. You must find a place for the kittens where Miss Rottenmeir will not see them. We do want to keep the little darlings, and play with them whenever we are alone. Where can you hide them?"

"I'll take care of them, Miss Klara, never fear," said Sebastian obligingly. "I'll give them a comfortable little basket and they shall not be found."

Sebastian picked up the kittens gently and went off with them, chuckling, for he liked to get the best of the house-keeper now and then.

The particular scolding that Miss Rottenmeier had reserved for Heidi had to wait until the next day, for the lady was much too exhausted for any disciplining that evening. She withdrew early, and the girls followed contentedly, knowing that their precious kittens were safe.

Chapter 8

WHEN THINGS DO NOT
GO SMOOTHLY

ON THE following morning, Sebastian had no sooner ushered the professor into the study, than the doorbell rang again, and with such authority that the butler flew downstairs, saying to himself, "That must be Mr. Sesemann himself. No one else rings like that."

He flung open the door and gaped at a ragged boy with a hand organ staring up at him.

"What do you mean, ringing the bell like that, like the master of the house himself! What do you want?" cried Sebastian wrathfully.

"I want to see Klara," was the answer, "whoever she is."

"You insolent streetboy! Can't you at least say *Miss* Klara? And what business could you possibly have with Miss Klara?" the butler asked, still more roughly.

"She owes me two marks," declared the lad.

"There must be something wrong with your head. How do you know Miss Klara?"

"I showed her the way yesterday, for one mark and the way back for another one which is two."

"Now what are you talking about? Miss Klara is an invalid. She never goes out. Be off with you!"

But the lad stood his ground. "I did see her yesterday in the street and I can tell you what she looks like. She has short black hair that curls, and her eyes are black, too, and her frock is brown."

"Oh, ho!" thought Sebastian, and chuckled. "That is clearly the little Mamselle. There has been more mischief!"

"Follow me," he told the lad, "And then wait at the

68

study door until you're allowed to enter. Once in, you are to play your organ; it will please Miss Klara."

Upstairs once more, Sebastian knocked at the study door and was told to enter. "There is a boy here who insists that he has something to say to Miss Klara herself," he announced. Klara looked suprised and delighted at this unusual occurrence.

"Let him come in," she said. "He may, may he not, Professor?"

But he was already in the room, and as directed, had begun to play.

Now, that morning Miss Rottenmeier was attending to things in the dining-room. All at once she stopped and listened. Could those sounds of a hand organ be coming from the study? Impossible! – yet there they were quite clearly. She flew through the long dining-room. And there – incredible! – there, in the middle of the study was a ragged boy, turning the handle of his hurdy-gurdy! The professor seemed to be trying to speak, without success. Klara and Heidi were listening, their faces beaming.

"Stop that dreadful noise at once!" cried Miss Rottenmeier, running towards the lad. Suddenly she felt something at her feet, and stooped to look on the floor. A horrid greyish, blackish animal was crawling under her skirts! It was a tortoise. Miss Rottenmeier leaped into the air, shrieking wildly, "Sebastian! Sebastian!"

The organ-grinder stopped and stared at her. Behind the half-open door, Sebastian was all doubled up with laughter. At last he entered. The housekeeper had sunk down into a chair, hand to her heart. "Drive them out! Both of them! At once! At once Sebastian."

The butler drew the lad out, complete with organ and tortoise, and pressed something into his hand, saying, "Two marks for Miss Klara, and two for the music. You did very well," whereupon he shut the house door.

In the study, quiet was restored and the lessons resumed. Miss Rottenmeier remained, to guard, if possible, against any new outbreak. She would investigate this matter and punish the wrongdoer in a way that would never be forgotten.

But now another knock sounded on the study door and Sebastian reappeared with the announcement that a large basket had just come, to be delivered to Miss Klara.

"To me?" exclaimed Klara in surprise. "Do let me see at once. Whatever can it be?"

Sebastian brought in the covered basket, and promptly withdrew.

"I think we will first finish our lessons and then inspect the basket," Miss Rottenmeier said.

But Klara could not keep her mind on her lessons. "Professor," she begged, "may I not take one look, only to see what there is in it?"

Before the professor could reply, the covering on the basket moved, and out leaped five little kittens! In a moment they seemed to be all over the whole room. One sat himself on the professor's boots and nibbled at his trousers. Another clambered up Miss Rottenmeier's dress, while a third sprang into Klara's lap. The housekeeper sat speechless, but Klara cried out in delight, "Oh, what adorable creatures! How they jump! Heidi! Look at this one! No, that!"

Heidi ran after them into all the corners, trying to gather them up. The professor stood by the table, hemming and hawing, quite unable to cope with the situation.

Miss Rottenmeier recovered her voice, and began to scream with all her might, *"Tinette! Sebastian!"*

At last the servants came running in, caught the kittens, one after another, and stuffed them into the basket. This they carried off to the attic, where the other kittens were secreted. During today's study hours, just as yesterday's, there had been no time for yawning.

Later that evening, when Miss Rottenmeier had recovered her spirits sufficiently, she summoned Sebastian and Tinette into the study, and began a thorough investigation into the occurrences of the afternoon. Thus she learned that it was Heidi who had arranged the whole affair.

The housekeeper went pale with anger. She dismissed the servants and turned to Heidi, who was standing beside Klara's chair with not the faintest idea of what crime she had committed.

"Adelheid," the housekeeper began in an ominous tone, "I know of only one punishment that may have some effect on you, for you are a barbarian. But we shall see if you do not become more civilized in our cellar with the rats and lizards."

Since Heidi had never been in a frightful cellar, she listened to all this without terror. However, Klara raised loud protests. "No, no, Miss Rottenmeier! We must wait until Papa comes. You know he will be here soon, and then after I have told him everything he will decide what is to be done with Heidi."

Against this proposal the housekeeper dared make no objection. She rose with a jerk and said crossly, "Very well, Klara! But I shall also have a word or two to say to your father." With that she sailed out of the room.

Klara, on the other hand, was quite content. With Heidi around the days were never dull.

But to Heidi, lesson time was no pleasure, for she always got the letters confused, no matter how the good professor explained them.

In the afternoons, after Klara had rested, Heidi sat beside her and told her endless tales of her life on the Alm. And, as she talked, her longing to return would become so great that she would say, "I really must go back tomorrow!"

Whenever she said this, Klara was able to soothe Heidi by saying that it would be better to wait until her father came. Heidi agreed, and was content enough because she had a secret project, and that was to collect a great heap of rolls for the goat-Peter's blind grandmother. That was the gift she had decided to take back with her. Therefore, morning and evening she added to her store the beautiful white roll that lay beside her plate, stuffing it quickly into her pocket.

Every day, after lunch, Heidi sat alone in her room for two long hours, for she now understood that she was not to go out by herself in Frankfurt, as if she were at home on the Alm. She was also forbidden to seek out Sebastian; and talking to Tinette never entered her head, for the lady's maid never spoke to her except mockingly.

So, sitting alone, Heidi had plenty of time to think of the Alm growing green again, and the yellow flowers glistening in the sunshine, and of how everything shone in the clear mountain air: the snow and the mountain – the whole valley. At times she felt as if she could not bear another moment away from her beloved Alm. Aunt Dete had assured her that she could go home whenever she wished. And so, one day the child could not restrain herself a moment longer. She packed all her rolls in her little shawl, put on her old straw hat, and started off.

But at the house door, Heidi met Miss Rottenmeier returning from a walk. The housekeeper stood still and stared blankly at the child. Then her gaze rested on the bulging red shawl.

"What does this mean?" she demanded. "Have I not forbidden you to run about the streets? Now you are at it again, and looking like a tramp into the bargain!"

"I am not going to run about in the streets. I am going home," Heidi answered, but she was frightened.

"What? Going home?" Miss Rottenmeier threw up her hands. "Do you mean you are running away? Oh, if Mr. Sesemann were to know this! Tell me, what is it that does not suit you here? Have you not been better treated than you deserve? Do you lack for anything? Have you ever in your life had so fine a home or food, or service? Speak up!"

"No," Heidi replied.

"I am sure of it," continued the housekeeper sternly, "You are the most ungrateful creature and full of mischief."

But Heidi had enough, and suddenly she burst out, "I

must go home and I will! I know that Snowball has been crying for me, and Thistlebird will be whipped because goat-Peter will have no more of my cheese. And here you can't see the sun say goodnight to the mountains, and if the eagle were to fly over Frankfurt, he would scream louder than ever to see so many people living so close together, and making each other wicked, instead of living on the mountain, and being happy."

"Merciful heaven! the child is mad!" Miss Rottenmeier screamed, rushing up the stairs and squarely into Sebastian, who was coming down.

"Carry that miserable child to her room at once," she ordered, getting her breath back.

Sebastian blinked his big round eyes and hurried to obey.

Heidi stood stock still below, her black eyes flashing, and trembling all over.

"What have you been up to now?" Sebastian asked her gaily. But then, taking a closer look, he patted her kindly on the shoulder as he said comfortingly, "The little Mamselle must not take it to heart, but we have to go upstairs. She has said so."

Her head low, and her heart even lower, Heidi went upstairs, slowly and heavily, not at all in her usual bouncy way. It hurt Sebastian to see her like this, and as they plodded along, he spoke encouragingly to her. "Don't give way now, Mamselle. Be brave! You have always been so sensible, never crying once since you have been here. The kittens have not cried, either. They play and romp in the attic, and are so funny. We'll go up there soon, when she is out of the house."

Heidi gave him so sorrowful a nod that it went straight to Sebastian's heart. Silently the child slipped into her own room.

At dinnertime the housekeeper said not a single word to the child, but she kept casting sharp glances at Heidi, as if she expected her to do something extraordinary. But Heidi sat like a mouse, and did not eat, or drink; although she did put away her roll quickly in her pocket as usual.

The next morning, when the professor came upstairs, Miss Rottenmeier motioned him into the dining-room and then told him of her anxiety regarding Heidi. How the change of air, she suggested, and the new way of living and strange surroundings might have affected the child's mind. She told him also of Heidi's attempt to run away, repeating as much of the child's wild conversation as she could recall.

The professor, however, assured her that he was convinced that although in some ways Adelheid was certainly a bit peculiar, in most ways she was perfectly normal. Little by little, and with careful education, the professor ventured, the necessary balance would be established. He did confess, however, that he found the situation rather difficult, because thus far he could not get Heidi beyond the ABC.

Somewhat calmer, Miss Rottenmeier released the professor to his duties. Later on, she thought of the strange costume in which Heidi had prepared to run away, and decided to alter some of Klara's dresses for the child. Heidi then would be properly dressed when Mr. Sesemann returned. Klara, when consulted, gladly gave a number of her dresses, jackets, and hats for Heidi's use.

The housekeeper next went to Heidi's bedroom to inspect her wardrobe, and decide what would be kept and what discarded. In a few minutes she returned, distressed and quite disgusted, to confront the child.

"What do you think I have now found, Adelheid?" she demanded. "Something never intended for a wardrobe, young lady! A pile of white rolls! Bread, Klara, and such a pile of it under the clothes! Tinette!" she cried, "remove all that dreadful stale bread from the wardrobe in Adelheid's room, and the old straw hat lying on the table, too."

"No, no!" Heidi exclaimed. "I want the hat, and the rolls are for Grandmother!" She tried to run after Tinette, but was caught by Miss Rottenmeier.

"Stay where you are," the housekeeper ordered, severely, "and all that rubbish must be thrown away."

Heidi crumpled on the floor by Klara's chair and wept, louder and louder, sobbing bitterly, "Now I'll have no rolls for Grandmother. They were all for her, all of them!" and she cried as if her heart would break.

Miss Rottenmeier held her head and ran out of the room, leaving Klara very much alarmed by the distress of her small friend.

"Heidi! Heidi!" she pleaded, "do not cry so. Listen! I promise I will give you just as many rolls as you had for the grandmother, and even more, when you go home. And they shall be fresh and soft, not hard and stale. Please, Heidi, listen, and don't cry any more! I can't bear to hear you."

But it was a long time before the torrent of sobs could be checked. Heidi understood what Klara said, and her promise was a comfort; otherwise she would have wept much longer.

Heidi came to dinner that evening with her eyes red from crying, and when she saw her usual roll, she began to sob again. But this time she controlled herself quickly.

Through the whole meal Sebastian made the most remarkable gestures every time he came into Heidi's view. He would point first to her head, then to his own, nod and wink as if to say, "Don't worry! I have looked after everything and it will be all right."

When Heidi went to her room, and was about to climb into bed, she found, tucked under the coverlet, her own straw hat. She pulled it out and hugged it tenderly, crumpling it even more. Then she wrapped it in a handkerchief and stuffed it in the darkest corner of her wardrobe. It was her friend, Sebastian, who had rescued the hat, Heidi knew, and that was what all the signs at dinner had meant.

Chapter 9

THE MASTER OF THE HOUSE

A FEW days later there was a great bustle about the house, for Mr. Sesemann had arrived. Tinette and Sebastian ran up and down the stairs, carrying parcels and boxes and yet more boxes and parcels, as the master of the house always brought with him a great quantity of beautiful things.

He, of course, went first of all into his daughter's room, where he found Heidi, sitting beside the invalid.

Klara greeted her father joyfully, for she loved him dearly, and he held her close with great tenderness. Then he turned, and stretched out his hand towards Heidi, who had withdrawn into a corner, saying, "And this, I suppose, is our little Swiss girl? Come, give me your hand, child. Now, tell me, are you and Klara good friends?"

"Oh yes! Klara is always good to me," Heidi said quickly.

"And Heidi never loses her temper," Klara added.

"That is good," Mr. Sesemann said. "Now I must have something to eat, but afterwards I shall come back, and you shall see what I have brought you."

Smiling at both girls, Mr. Sesemann went into the dining-room, where the housekeeper awaited him. He took his seat, and she sat opposite him, with a face so long and gloomy, that presently he said, "My dear Miss Rotten-meier, is something wrong?"

"Mr. Sesemann," the housekeeper began earnestly, "we have been dreadfully deceived."

"Indeed? How?" asked the gentleman.

Miss Rottenmeier sighed. "We had, as you know, de-cided to secure a playmate for Klara, someone to live here with us. Knowing how particular you are, I set my mind on finding an ideal Swiss child, one bred upon pure mountain air, who would, so to speak, walk through life without touching the earth."

"I think," said Mr. Sesemann, trying to keep his lips from twitching, "that the Swiss also touch the earth. Otherwise they would have wings."

"Mr. Sesemann, I am not jesting," Miss Rottenmeier said reproachfully. "Indeed, this is more serious a matter than you suspect. I have been grossly, oh most fearfully deceived."

"But how? I see nothing in the child that is so dreadful."

"Oh, sir! I'll tell you *one* thing. The child has brought into your house the strangest men and beasts, and the professor can bear me out."

"Beasts? I do not understand this, Miss Rottenmeier!"

"Who can! The behaviour of this girl is beyond understanding – unless of course, she is mentally unbalanced."

Up to this point, Klara's father had been more amused than concerned, but now, he gazed steadily at his housekeeper, as if to assure himself that she was not the person mentally afflicted. At this moment, the professor was announced.

"Ah, here comes our learned friend. Perhaps he will explain this mystery!" cried Mr. Sesemann, and quite gladly. "Come! Be seated. A cup of coffee for the professor, please, Miss Rottenmeier," the master of the house said, shaking the newcomer's hand. "Tell me," he then continued, "about the child who has come as a companion for my daughter. What is this about her bringing animals into the house? And is there anything the matter with her mind? Do you think she should remain as a companion to my daughter?"

The professor pursed his learned lips and made a steeple of his thin fingers. "Well, Mr. Sesemann," he began, "I should not like to be thrown too much with the child myself, for she is, on the one side, quite inexperienced socially, which, of course, is the case with the less civilized wild beings with whom this child has lived until she came to Frankfurt, but this, to be sure, will change and then –"

Obviously it would take the dear professor the better part of the day to get to the point, Mr. Sesemann realized, and he determined to conduct his own investigation. "Excuse me, Professor," he said hastily. "Pray do not disturb yourself. I must go to my daughter for a moment."

Mr. Sesemann made his escape, and did not reappear again. Joining his daughter in the study, he sat down beside her, and wishing to get Heidi out of the room, said, "My dear, won't you bring me a glass of water?"

"Fresh water?" asked Heidi.

"Yes, yes; nice and fresh."

Heidi's head bobbed and she disappeared.

"Now, Klara, darling," said her father taking her hand in his, "tell me what sort of animals has your playmate brought into the house? And what makes Miss Rottenmeier think the child may be not quite right in her mind?"

Since the housekeeper had repeated to Klara some of Heidi's "wild" talk – which Klara had understood perfectly – she was able to explain to her father all that had happened, the matter of the tortoise and the kittens, and Heidi's outburst on the doorstep. Whereupon Mr. Sesemann laughed heartily.

"Then you don't wish the child sent away, do you, Klara? You are not weary of her?" he asked.

"No, Papa, no indeed! Please don't think of sending her away! Since Heidi's been here something new keeps happening every day. It is quite different here from what it used to be. Then nothing ever happened. Besides, Heidi tells me so many interesting things."

"Very well, child. Here comes your little friend again. Well, and have you brought me some nice fresh water?"

"Yes, sir," the child replied politely, extending a sparkling glass.

"Did you bring it all the way from the fountain yourself, Heidi?" asked Klara.

78

"Yes, I did, it is quite fresh; but I had to go a long way to get it. There were so many people at the first fountain, that I went up the street, and then there were too many by the next one. Then I turned into another street, and there I got the water; and a gentleman with white hair sends his compliments to Mr. Sesemann."

"Well, now, the expedition was a successful one," laughed Mr. Sesemann. "But who was the gentleman?"

"He was passing by the fountain, and he stopped and said: 'Since you have a glass, will you give me some water to drink? Pray, who are you getting the water for?' And I said, 'For Mr. Sesemann'. Then he laughed very hard, and said he hoped you would enjoy it."

"Well, who was it that wished to be remembered to me? How did he look?"

"He looked pleasant, and he had a thick gold chain, and a gold thing hung from it with a big red stone, and on his walking stick was a horse's head."

"That is the doctor. That is my old doctor," said Mr. Sesemann and his daughter in the same breath. And Mr. Sesemann laughed quietly to himself, over his friend's reflections as to his new way of getting his supply of water.

That evening, Mr. Sesemann told Miss Rottenmeier that he found Heidi quite normal and without any mental disorders. Therefore, he wished for the child to remain in his house as Klara's companion. Heidi pleased his daughter and made her happy – and that was that.

"I also wish," Mr. Sesemann continued with still more decision, "to have the child treated most kindly, and I do not want any of her peculiarities to be considered as misconduct. You will not have to manage her alone for long, Miss Rottenmeier, as my mother will be here soon to make an extended visit. As you know, my mother can manage anybody if she sets her mind on it."

"Yes, indeed. I know that very well, Mr. Sesemann," the housekeeper replied, but not with any great enthusiasm at the prospect.

Mr. Sesemann's stay with his daughter was to be a short one this time. He was obliged to return to Paris at the end of a fortnight. However, he cheered Klara with the promise of the speedy arrival of her grandmamma, who was expected in a few days.

Almost as soon as Mr. Sesemann left, a letter came from Holstein, where the grandmamma lived on an old family estate, saying that she would arrive on the following day.

Klara, overjoyed, then told Heidi so much about her wonderful grandmamma, that the child began to call the lady by the same name. This brought her strong glares of disapproval from Miss Rottenmeier and later she was summoned by the housekeeper and told sternly never to use the word "Grandmamma" again, but always to address Mrs. Sesemann as "gracious lady."

"Do you understand me?" Miss Rottenmeier asked, seeing that Heidi looked rather doubtful. She gave the child such a frown that Heidi nodded, even though she still thought "Gracious" was an odd name for anybody – even Klara's grandmamma.

Chapter 10

A GRANDMAMMA

FROM the busy preparations that went on, the day that Mrs. Sesemann was to arrive, it was clear the lady commanded the greatest respect in the household. Tinette wore a fine new white cap for the occasion, and Sebastian arranged a great number of footstools, and put them before every chair and couch, so that the lady might find one wherever she chose to sit. Even the housekeeper went through the rooms, setting everything in order with her own hands.

At last the carriage rolled up to the house. Tinette and

Sebastian hurried down the stairs. Miss Rottenmeier followed with great dignity.

Heidi had been ordered to her own room, to wait until she was sent for, as the grandmamma would naturally hasten to Klara and wish to be alone with her, the housekeeper said. Seated in her bedroom, Heidi repeated over and over the strange way in which she was to address Mrs. Sesemann. Always before she had heard the title placed before the name and not after. Presently she decided that Miss Rottenmeier must have been excited and so made a mistake. Heidi turned the words about and they seemed more sensible.

Tinette soon appeared, and with her usual shortness, announced, "You are wanted in the study."

As Heidi opened the door, she heard the grandmamma's friendly voice, "Ah, here comes the child! Come to me, dear, and let me look at you."

Heidi walked up to the lady in her clear voice, said "Good day, Lady Gracious."

The grandmamma's eyes twinkled. "Do they say that where you come from on the Alm, little one?"

"No, no one there has a name like that," the child replied seriously.

"Nor here, either," Mrs. Sesemann said pleasantly, patting the child on the cheek. "Here I am always Grandmamma, and you must call me so, too. Will you remember that?"

"Oh, yes! I did call you that before," Heidi said.

"I understand, now!" Grandmamma nodded, much amused. She studied the little girl for some time, nodding again in approval, and Heidi, looking straight into the kind eyes, felt quite happy. Grandmamma had such soft white hair, and on her head was a beautiful lace cap, twisted with two wide ribbons that kept moving a little as if a breeze stirred about her.

"What is your name, child?" the lady asked.

"My name is Heidi, but if I must be called Adelheid, I

will try to remember it," she said earnestly, for she did not always remember when Miss Rottenmeier called her by that name.

As she said the words the housekeeper entered. "Mrs. Sesemann will doubtless agree," said she, "that I must use the real name that was given you."

"My good Rottenmeier," said Mrs. Sesemann, "there is nothing wrong with the name of Heidi. If the child has been accustomed to it, I shall certainly use it, and no other."

The housekeeper did not like to be called by her simple name, without a preceding title, but the grandmamma had her own way of setting people down – when they needed it. It had taken her but a moment to see what was amiss with the child.

On the day after her arrival, while Klara took her daily rest, the old lady suddenly decided to visit Miss Rottenmeier, so she went to the housekeeper's room, and knocked. Miss Rottenmeier appeared, and was very much startled at the sight of this unexpected visitor.

"Where does the child stay while Klara naps, and what does she do?" Mrs. Sesemann asked without wasting words.

"She sits in her room, where she might employ herself in something useful if she wished. But instead, Mrs. Sesemann, she thinks up all sorts of mad projects and, worse, often carries them out too," the housekeeper replied in an aggrieved voice.

"That is precisely what I should do, too, if I were obliged to sit alone as that child does!" Mrs. Sesemann declared. "Go now and bring the child to my room, where I have some pretty books that I shall give her to read."

"Ah, but that is the most miserable thing of all," cried Miss Rottenmeier. "In all this time she has not learned even the alphabet. The professor can tell you all about that. If that man did not have the patience of an angel, he would have given up the lessons long ago."

"That's strange," Mrs. Sesemann said. "The little girl

does not strike me as a child who could not learn her letters. Go and get her; she can at least enjoy the pictures."

Miss Rottenmeier was not through recounting Heidi's faults, but Mrs. Sesemann was already moving briskly towards her own room. She was greatly surprised at this account of the child's backwardness, and determined to find out for herself what it meant.

Heidi came into Grandmamma's room eagerly and opened her eyes wide when she saw all the beautiful pictures in the big books that Grandmamma showed her. All at once she cried out as a page was turned, and then burst into loud sobs. Grandmamma studied the picture. It showed a beautiful green field, where sheep and goats were feeding. In their midst stood the shepherd leaning on his staff. Everything in the little scene was flooded with a shining, golden radiance, for the sun was just sinking beyond the horizon.

Putting her arms round the child, Grandmamma said soothingly, "Come now, my dear, don't cry. This picture has reminded you of something. But look, here is a story all about the picture. I will read it to you this evening. There are sorts of stories in this book that one can read. But now let us have a little talk together. There, dry your eyes so that I can look at you. Yes, that's better."

It was some time, however, before the shuddering little sobs stopped altogether. Then the grandmamma said, "Now tell me, child, how do you like to study with the professor? Do you learn easily?"

"Oh, no," Heidi answered sighing, "but I knew beforehand that I couldn't."

"And why not, child?"

"Some people just can't learn to read. It's too hard."

"Really! and how did you discover a thing like that?"

"Peter told me, and he knows very well. He never can learn, because it's too hard."

"Then this Peter must be a strange fellow! You must not take for granted that which such a Peter says is so – because, certainly, this is not. Possibly, because of this very Peter you have not given close attention to what the Professor says, and have not looked closely at the letters. Believe me, you *can* learn to read, and quickly, too, as all children do who are like you, and not like Peter.

"Now, as soon as you have learned to read, you shall have this book with the shepherd and the green meadow for your very own. Then you can learn the whole story just as if someone told it to you, all about his sheep and goats, and the wonderful things that happen to him and them."

Heidi, who had listened with rapt attention, exclaimed, "Oh, if I could only read right now!"

"That will come soon enough. You will only have to try. But now we must go to Klara, and we will take the books with us."

Heidi had changed a great deal since the day when Miss Rottenmeier had stopped her from running away. The housekeeper had told her then that she was an ungrateful child, and that Mr. Sesemann must never know about it. Now Heidi understood that she could not go home again whenever she wished, as Aunt Dete had assured her she could, and that Mr. Sesemann would be displeased with her if he ever learned that she wished to go. She reasoned in her own mind that Klara and her grandmamma would feel the same way about it. So she did not tell anyone of her longing for the mountains for fear of making Grandmamma, whom she already loved dearly, as angry as Miss Rottenmeier had been.

So Heidi's heart became heavier and heavier. She lost her appetite and she grew paler every day. At night she often lay awake for a long time, for as soon as she put her head upon the pillow, the Alm and the sunshine upon it, and the flowers, came vividly before her eyes. When she at last fell asleep, the red pinnacles filled her dreams, and she awakened full of joy, ready to spring out of bed, and run out of the hut – until she realized that she was in Frankfurt, far, far from her beloved home, and she could not get back!

Then Heidi buried her face in her pillow and cried, but quietly, so that no one could hear her.

Her unhappiness, however, did not escape the attentive eyes of Mrs. Sesemann. The good lady allowed several days to pass, to see if Heidi might recover her high spirits, but the child continued to droop, and her red eyes often betrayed her weeping. One day Grandmamma took Heidi into her room again, and said gently, "Tell me, child, what is troubling you?"

But Heidi could not tell her, for then Grandmamma would know what an ungrateful child she had before her, and she would lose her love. So Heidi hung her head and said, "It isn't anything that I can tell."

"Not even Klara?"

"No. Not anybody!" Heidi declared so miserably that Mrs. Sesemann's heart ached for the child.

"When one has a sorrow that cannot be told to anybody on earth, it must be confided to God, and He must be asked for help and comfort. He can make our sorrows lighter and teach us to bear them. You pray to the dear Father in heaven every evening, don't you?"

"No, I never do," Heidi said.

"Have you never learned to pray?"

"Oh, yes. With my first grandmother I did. But that was long ago, and I've forgotten about it."

"I see now why you are so unhappy, Heidi. It is because you have not asked the good Lord to help you."

Heidi gazed at Grandmamma hopefully. "Can you tell God everything?"

"Everything, Heidi."

"May I go, then?" the child asked breathlessly, and ran quickly to her room.

Seated on her footstool, with her hands folded, she told all the sorrow of her heart to God and begged him to help her get home again, to her grandfather on the Alm.

About a week later the professor asked permission to see Mrs. Sesemann regarding an important matter. He was invited to her room, and the lady greeted him cordially saying, "My dear Professor, I am delighted to see you. Do be seated here beside me. There now, tell me what brings you here. Nothing unpleasant I trust?"

"On the contrary, Madam, it is something most extraordinarily pleasant."

"Has Heidi learned to read, Professor?"

The astonished gentleman stared at Mrs. Sesemann in surprise. How had she guessed?

"It is truly remarkable," said he, finding his voice. "I had decided to give up trying to teach this child when all at once, overnight, so to speak, she has begun to read, and with a correctness rare among beginners."

Mrs Sesemann smiled with satisfaction. "Sometimes, Professor, a new desire to learn is born along with a new approach to teaching. Let us rejoice that the child has begun so well, and hope she will continue to make good progress."

With this she accompanied the professor to the door, and straight to the study, to confirm the pleasant news.

It was all true. Heidi sat by Klara's side, reading a story, and with growing eagerness exploring this new world that had suddenly opened before her.

That very evening, when Heidi took her seat at table, there, on her plate, lay the beautiful book Grandmamma had promised to give her.

"Is it mine forever? Even when I go home?" asked Heidi.

"Yes, certainly, forever," Grandmamma replied.

"But you won't go home for many years yet, Heidi!" exclaimed Klara. "My grandmamma will be going away and you must stay with me."

That night before she went to sleep, Heidi looked at the new book in her own room. Always thereafter, it was her favourite to read and re-read countless times.

Whenever the grandmamma suggested, "Now Heidi read something to us," the child was delighted, for she read quite easily now.

Her favourite picture was the green pasture, with the shepherd and his flock. He took care of the sheep and goats, and he loved them. But the next picture showed him after he had run away from his father's home into a foreign land, where he was forced to feed swine. Here he had grown quite thin for he had very little to eat. In this picture the sun was not golden, and the land was grey and barren. One other picture belonged to this story. There the old father came running from his house to welcome the repentant son, who came back gaunt and ragged, and yet was not less beloved.

This was the story Heidi liked best, and she never tired of hearing Mrs. Sesemann explain it to her and Klara.

The days passed all too quickly, and soon it would be time for the dear grandmamma to return to her own home. This was something Heidi did not like to think about.

Chapter 11

HOMESICKNESS

DURING Klara's afternoon rest, Grandmamma usually seated herself beside her, and dozed for a while also. Miss Rottenmeier, however, disappeared into her own room. But Grandmamma's nap was short, and she always called Heidi in, to talk to her or occupy her in various ways. She had a quantity of pretty dolls with her, and bits and pieces of bright coloured cloth which she showed Heidi how to make into dresses and aprons for them. Heidi learned to sew quickly, and made the prettiest dolls clothes with tiny stitches.

But although she could read and sew, and even though she had Grandmamma's love and kindest attention, Heidi was never really happy as before, and her black eyes no longer sparkled with joy.

During the last week of Mrs. Sesemann's stay in Frankfurt, she called Heidi into her room and studying the child gravely, said, "Tell me, dear Heidi, why are you unhappy? Do you still have the same trouble in your heart?"

"Yes," the child replied.

"Have you asked God to help you?"

"Yes."

"And do you pray to him every night?"

"No, not any more now."

"What? Do I hear you right, Heidi? Why don't you pray now?"

"It didn't do any good. The Lord did not listen."

"How can you be sure of that?"

"I have asked for the same thing every night for weeks and God has not given it to me."

"But that is not so, child. The good God always knows what is best for us, though we may not know ourselves. If what we pray for is not good for us, He does not grant it. Instead He sends us something better – if we continue to pray to Him. You must believe that the thing you prayed for is not good for you now, and you must not stop praying. Instead you should ask God for forgiveness, and put your trust in Him, and He will do what is good for you, and make you happy again."

Heidi had listened intently to every word that Grandmamma said and each one fell deep into her heart, for she had perfect faith in her kind friend.

"I will go at once," she said, "and beg God to forgive me and I will never forget Him again."

The day for Mrs. Sesemann's departure came at last, and a sad time it was for the two girls. The grandmamma tried to make it as cheerful as possible, but when her carriage rolled off, such a feeling of loneliness swept over the children that they did not know what to do with themselves.

After lessons the next day, Heidi brought her precious

book under her arm, saying, "Would you like me to read to you, Klara?"

Klara nodded, and Heidi began at once. But unfortunately Heidi began with a story about a sick and dying grandmother, and all at once she began to cry in great distress, for somehow she took it into her head that everything she read was true, and now she thought that it was the blind grandmother in Dorfli who was dying.

"Grandmother is dead," she sobbed, "and I never got to see her, or to bring her a single roll of white bread!"

Klara did her best to comfort Heidi, and to explain that the story had nothing whatever to do with the grandmother on the Alm. But Heidi was sure that while she was so far away, her grandfather might die, too! And then she would not have anyone to live with on the Alm.

While Heidi wept and wailed, Miss Rottenmeier came into the room, and heard Klara's efforts to quiet her small companion. But as Heidi could not control her tears, the housekeeper at last said most decidedly, "Adelheid, this senseless noise has gone on long enough. Stop it at once, and, if you ever again burst out crying in this way over a story, I will take your book from you, and you shall never have it again."

This had an instantaneous effect. Heidi turned white with terror: the book was her dearest treasure. She dried her eyes and swallowed sobs, so that she made no sound. Never again did she cry aloud, no matter what she read, but sometimes the effort to control herself was so violent that Klara would look at her, quite astonished, and ask, "Why are you making such frightful faces, Heidi?"

At any rate the faces made no noise, and Miss Rottenmeier did not happen to see any of them.

With all this agitation, however, Heidi grew paler and thinner every day. Sebastian was most distressed as she constantly passed up the daintiest morsels and scarcely nibbled at the food on her plate. And when Heidi lay down on her pillow at night, she cried herself to sleep with homesickness.

And so the long unhappy days passed by. Heidi scarcely knew whether it was summer or winter, for walls and windows always looked the same. The only time she went out was when Klara was feeling especially well, and could take a drive. But these drives were always very short, for even the slightest exertion fatigued the delicate girl. Therefore they rarely drove beyond the tall houses and paved streets, where no grass or flowers, or pine trees or mountains were visible. And Heidi's longing for these accustomed sights grew so strong, that sometimes she felt she could not bear it another moment without a fit of crying. But she managed to save this for her pillow, where Miss Rottenmeier would neither see nor hear her.

So the winter went by, and the sun shone so dazzlingly upon the white walls opposite the Sesemann house that Heidi knew it was time for goat-Peter to go up to the mountain pasture with his flock. And there the golden buttercups would glisten in the sunshine, and in the evening everything would glow with a warm rosy light. Then she would sit in a corner of her lonely bedroom and hold her small thin hands over her eye so that she could not see the sunshine on the wall, and she would sit there motionless, stifling her homesickness, until Klara sent for her.

Chapter 12

THE HOUSE IS HAUNTED

AT ABOUT this time, Miss Rottenmeier took to wandering about the house wrapped in thoughtful silence. Towards evening, when she had to go from one room to another through the long corridors, she looked around her nervously, as if she expected someone to sneak up behind her and jerk at her dress, without being seen. When it grew dark, she did not go about alone except in the rooms where the family lived. If she had business upstairs, in the handsomely furnished guest rooms, or in the lower part of the house, where the great hall was where every step awakened mysterious echoes, and Sesemann ancestors stared down from their portraits on the walls she always called for Tinette, pretending there might be something to carry up or down.

Tinette, in her turn, did the same thing, only she called Sebastian to accompany her in case there were something heavy to be moved.

Strangest of all, Sebastian, too, required company, if he had to go to a distant part of the great house. He called on John, the coachman, to come with him, to help in whatever way might be necessary. Each responded to the other's call willingly, although there was never anything to bring up or down, push or pull. It was as if each one thought he might need some sort of help.

While all this was happening above stairs, the old cook stood amid her pots and pans shaking her head and sighing, as she said woefully, "To think that I should live to see such goings-on here, in this house!"

For something very strange indeed had been taking place in the Sesemann home. Every morning when the servants came downstairs, the house door stood wide open, and no one could account for it. The first time this occurred, every corner was searched for fear that something had been stolen. Quite naturally everyone thought that a thief had hidden himself in the house, and then escaped with his loot in the night. But nothing appeared to be stolen; not a thing in the whole house was missing.

Thereafter, at night, the door was not only double-locked, but fastened across with a stout wooden beam. It did no good. In the morning, the door stood wide open; and no matter how early the servants might come downstairs, there was the door, flung wide, although everyone in the neighbourhood was asleep, and all the other doors were closed tight.

At last, urged and encouraged by Miss Rottenmeier, Sebastian and John decided to spend the night in the room that opened into the great hall, and thus try to unravel the mystery.

The pair armed themselves with clubs and prepared to wait for whatever might be coming. However, it was dull waiting in the dark, and soon both men were fast asleep. When the church tower clock struck twelve, Sebastian roused himself, and called to his companion, but though John wakened, he soon went to sleep again.

Sebastian was now very wide awake, and listening to every sound. All was still.

At about one o'clock, John suddenly awoke and remembered why he was in a chair, and not in his bed. All at once he felt brave. "Let's see what is going on," he said, rising to light the lamp on the table between them. "Don't be afraid. You may come behind me," he added, turning down the wick.

The door of their room had been left ajar, and now, as John gave it a push, both men felt a sharp draught of air coming from the open house door. The gust was so strong that it put out the lamp John held, and as he started back with a jerk, he nearly knocked Sebastian off his feet.

John shut their door with a whoosh, and turned the key in the lock. Then he pulled out his matches and lighted the lamp again. Sebastian did not rightly know what had happened, but, when he saw his companion by the lamplight, he cried out in alarm. John was white as chalk, and shaking like an aspen leaf.

"What did you see out there?" asked Sebastian anxiously.

"The door, wide open," John croaked, "and on the steps, a white figure, going down. Whist! and it disappeared."

A cold chill ran down Sebastian's back. Now the two men huddled together in terror, and did not stir again until it was bright daylight. Then they crept out, closed the front door that had stood wide all this time, and hurried to tell Miss Rottenmeier what had happened.

The housekeeper had scarcely slept for fear of what might be going on downstairs. As soon as she heard what they had seen, she dismissed the men, and flew to write Mr. Sesemann a distracted letter, saying that he must come home without delay, for most unheard-of things were taking place. She recounted what had happened, and assured the master of the house that matters were so grave that nobody in the household felt secure, and it was impossible to foretell what might occur next.

Mr. Sesemann, however, did not rush home. Instead he replied it was impossible for him to drop everything at such short notice. The ghost story was absurd, and he hoped that the excitement would soon pass. In the meanwhile, he felt sure Miss Rottenmeier could handle the ridiculous situation, whatever it might be.

Miss Rottenmeier was not pleased by the tone of this letter. Moreover she was not inclined to spend her days and nights in terror. She knew precisely what she should do. Up to now she had refrained from telling the children about the ghost for fear that they would insist on her remaining with them day and night, which would not be very convenient to her. Now she marched straight into the study, and told them of the mysterious apparition, speaking in a hushed, frightened way.

As expected, Klara declared at once that she would not be left alone for a moment. Papa must be sent for, and Miss Rottenmeier must come to sleep in her room. Heidi must not be left alone either, so they would all sleep in one room. The light must be left burning all night and Tinette must also sleep near by. Sebastian and John must stay in the corridor, to shout and frighten the ghost away, if they saw it coming.

Klara was so upset that the housekeeper could scarcely quieten her. She promised, indeed, to write to Mr. Sesemann at once and to have her bed set up in Klara's room, and not to leave her alone at night. If Adelheid were afraid, too, Tinette could sleep with her.

But Heidi would rather face a ghost than Tinette; and besides she'd never heard of ghosts before, so she said at once that she was not afraid and did not need company.

Miss Rottenmeier did not waste a moment. Again a letter went off to Mr. Sesemann. The mysterious happenings in the house were affecting the health of his delicate daughter and who could tell what the consequences might be? Certainly these nightly alarms were not doing his Klara any good, and so on, and so on. . .

This letter brought results. Two days later, Mr. Sesemann pulled the door bell with such violence that the servants stared at each other in alarm. Was it possible that now the ghost had become so bold it had begun to play tricks in broad daylight?

Sebastian peeped out through an upper window, recognized his master, and took off at a gallop to open the door as quickly as possible.

Mr. Sesemann greeted Sebastian shortly, and went straight to his daughter's room. Her joyful welcome reassured him somewhat and when she told him that she felt well, and almost fond of the ghosts, for without it she would not have him with her now, her father relaxed entirely.

"And pray, what further pranks is our ghost up to now, Miss Rottenmeier?" asked Mr. Sesemann, the corners of his mouth twitching.

"Sir, this is no joking matter," the housekeeper said solemnly. "Tomorrow morning you will see for yourself, and you will not laugh then."

Mr. Sesemann sighed. "Very well, Miss Rottenmeier. Now please call Sebastian into the dining-room. I wish to speak with him."

In the dining-room, the master of the house studied Sebastian closely. "Look here, my man," he said. "Tell me honestly. Is there some trick being played on Miss Rottenmeier?"

"No! on my word, sir." Sebastian appeared genuinely shocked. "In truth, sir, I feel rather uncomfortable about the thing myself."

"Indeed. In that case, I'll have to show such brave fellows as Sebastian and John how ghosts look by daylight.

"Now, go at once to my old friend, Dr. Classen, and ask that he come to me without fail at nine o'clock this evening. I have come from Paris especially to consult him. He must plan to spend the night with me, for it is a serious matter. Do you understand?"

"Perfectly, sir. Have no fear, I shall deliver the message correctly."

At nine o'clock, precisely, just as the children and Miss Rottenmeier withdrew for the night, the good doctor appeared. He was a pink-faced gentleman, with bright and kindly eyes that appeared anxious at the moment. However, after greeting his friend, he said, "You do not look as if you were in need of a doctor's watching, sir!"

"Only be patient, friend," Mr. Sesemann said. "The person for whom we are to watch will be a serious case when we have captured him."

"What's this? Someone ailing in the house who must be caught?" The doctor was quite puzzled.

"Far worse, sir. We have a ghost in the house! We are haunted!

Dr. Classen threw back his head and laughed.

"That is a fine way for you to take my shocking news. It is a pity Miss Rottenmeier is not here to reprimand you as she did me earlier. She is convinced we have a ghost wandering about here."

"Indeed?" the doctor still was much amused.

Mr. Sesemann then told his friend the story, and added that he was prepared for whatever they discovered. He had two loaded pistols, for he believed the affair was either a bad joke played on the household by some acquaintance of the servants, in which case a shot or two in the air would do no harm. Or, there might really be a thief, who wished to establish the idea of a ghost in order to pursue his looting undisturbed. In that case a good weapon would be useful.

During the explanation, the gentlemen descended the stairs, and went into the room where John and Sebastian had passed their eventful night. On the table stood a tray of refreshments, and beside it lay the revolvers. Two candlesticks, each holding an array of lighted candles, stood there also, for Mr. Sesemann had no intention of waiting for the ghost in the dark.

The door was partly shut to prevent too much light from shining into the corridor and frightening the ghost away. The two gentlemen seated themselves comfortably and prepared to wait, entertaining themselves with stories, and the refreshments thoughtfully provided for them. When twelve o'clock sounded, they were amazed, for they had not thought it to be so late.

"The ghost knows we are here and will not show itself tonight," remarked the doctor.

"It does not walk until one," his friend replied.

They laughed and went on talking. One o'clock sounded.

96

The house was still; not a sound was heard. Suddenly the doctor raised his finger.

The two men listened intently. Softly, but quite clearly, they heard the bar from the house door being moved. The key turned in the lock and the door was opened.

"You are not afraid?" asked the doctor, rising.

"It is best to be cautious," whispered Mr. Sesemann, taking a candlestick in one hand and a revolver in the other. The doctor, similarly equipped, had gone before him. Quickly they stepped into the corridor.

A white figure stood motionless in the moonlight, on the threshold of the wide-open house door.

"Who goes there?" the doctor thundered, and with lights and weapons brandished, both gentlemen approached the figure.

It turned about and uttered a cry. There stood little Heidi, in her white nightgown and bare feet, staring with dazzled eyes at the bright lights and revolvers, and quivering from head to foot.

"I do believe this is your daughter's playmate," gasped the doctor.

"Dear child, what does this mean? Why have you come down here?" asked Mr. Sesemann wonderingly.

Pale with fright, Heidi whispered, "I don't know."

The doctor stepped forward. "Sesemann," said he "this is a case for me. Go to your armchair. I'll take the child back where she belongs." Laying his revolver aside, he took the trembling little hand, and with fatherly tenderness led her upstairs.

"Don't be afraid," he said kindly, as they ascended. "There is nothing to fear."

In Heidi's room, he set down his light, took the child in his arms, put her into bed, and covered her up carefully. Then, seating himself beside her, he waited patiently until her trembling had subsided. Then, taking Heidi's hand in his, he said soothingly, "There, everything is all right again. Now, tell me where you were going?"

"I wasn't going anywhere," Heidi said. "I didn't go down there myself. I was there all at once."

"Really? Tell me, child, did you dream anything? Do you remember seeing or hearing anything very clearly?"

"Every night I dream the same dream. I think I am with my grandfather, and I hear the wind singing in the pines, and the stars are shining in the sky. I jump up and run to open the door of the hut, and oh, it is so beautiful! But when I awaken, I am always in Frankfurt." And Heidi began to gulp and try to swallow the sobs that filled her little throat almost to bursting.

"Hm. Have you any pain, anywhere? In your back or your head?"

"No, only here like a big stone all the time." Heidi placed her hand on her chest. "As if I *must* cry."

"And do you cry very hard?"

"Oh, no! I don't cry. Miss Rottenmeier has forbidden it."

"So you swallow it down until the next time, eh? I understand. You like it here in Frankfurt, don't you?"

"Oh, yes!" she replied, but very faintly, and it sounded as if she meant exactly the opposite.

"Hm. Where did you live with your grandather, child?"

"Always on the Alm."

"That couldn't have been so very pleasant. In fact, rather dreary, I would say."

"Oh, no! It was beautiful! beautiful!" Heidi could contain herself no more. All the longing, the excitement of the last half-hour, the long pent-up tears, overpowered her and she burst into loud sobs.

The doctor smoothed the child's hair, saying gently, "Yes, cry now. It will do you good. Then go to sleep, and tomorrow everything will be all right." Then he rose and left the room.

Downstairs again, the doctor seated himself in the armchair opposite his anxious host.

"In the first place, Sesemann," he said, "of course you

realize that your little *protégée* walks in her sleep. Quite unconsciously she has played the ghost, opened your house door every night, and frightened your servants out of their wits. In the second place, the child is suffering from such homesickness that she is reduced almost to a skeleton, and soon will be one, if this goes on. Something must be done for her at once. For the first trouble, and her extremely nervous state, there is only one cure; and that is to send the child back to her native mountains. For the second, she needs the same thing – her home. My prescription: send the child home tomorrow."

Mr. Sesemann leaned his head on his hands, then sprang from his chair to walk rapidly up and down the room. At last he said, "A sleepwalker! sick! homesick! wasted away to a skeleton – and in my house, Classen! All this in my house! And nobody noticed! And you, doctor, you wish that this child, who came to us fresh and healthy should be sent back to her grandfather faded and ailing? Never! Do what you think best, but cure her. Then I will send her back home whenever she wishes, but first you must help her get well."

"Sesemann," replied Dr. Classen gravely. "Think! This condition is not an illness to be cured by pills and tonics. The child is not of a naturally robust constitution; but if she is allowed to return to the bracing mountain air which she needs – desperately, she will become strong again. Sesemann, you would not have her return to her grandfather beyond all help – or never return at all, would you?"

Shocked, Mr. Sesemann stared at the grave-faced doctor.

"If that is your advice, Classen, there is no choice," he said at last, heavily. "It must be done as you say. Immediately."

He took his friend's arm and they walked up and down the long room. When the master of the house opened the door to let the doctor out, the bright sunlight streamed in.

Chapter 13

A SUMMER EVENING ON THE ALM

AFTER the doctor left, Mr. Sesemann climbed the stairs rapidly to the housekeeper's room, and knocked loudly at her door. Miss Rottenmeier uttered a cry of alarm and then heard the master's voice, saying imperiously, "Make haste, please, and come to the dining-room without delay. Preparations for a journey must be made immediately."

Miss Rottenmeier blinked as she looked at her clock. It was only half past four in the morning. She had never been out of bed this early in her life. What could have happened? Considerably agitated, she fumbled into her clothes every which way, buttoning all the buttons wrong and having to do them all over again.

In the meantime, Mr. Sesemann went through the hall and pulled every bell with all his might, to call each of the servants. Such a jumping up out of bed and a hurrying to dress followed. Everyone believed that the ghost had laid violent hands on the watchers, and that this somehow was their call for help. Down they galloped, one after the other, each looking worse than the last, and stood in astonishment before their master, who looked fresh and lively, and not in the least frightened by anything.

John was told to get the carriage ready. Tinette was to awaken and dress Heidi at once, for the child was to be prepared for an immediate journey. Sebastian was sent to the house where Dete lived, to bring her without delay to Mr. Sesemann.

Miss Rottenmeier appeared at last, panting a bit from exertion and curiosity. With scarcely a glance at her, Mr. Sesemann requested her to prepare a trunk for the little Swiss (so he always spoke of Heidi), and to place in it a good quantity of Klara's clothing, so that the child should have what was necessary to take with her, and to do this without delay.

Beyond this, much to Miss Rottenmeier's disappointment, Mr. Sesemann gave not a word of explanation. Leaving her to follow his instructions, he went to his daughter's bedroom. As he expected, Klara was wide awake, and trying vainly to guess what was going on in the house at this unusual hour.

Seating himself on her bed, her father told her who their ghost really was and that little Heidi, in Dr. Classen's opinion, was on the verge of serious illness. Moreover, she would probably continue her nightly wanderings, which might prove to be very dangerous, should she sometime take a misstep in her sleep. It was therefore necessary to send the little girl home to her grandfather in the mountains, for she would never get well again if she were kept in Frankfurt.

At first Klara could not believe that matters were as serious as he said. She did not wish to be deprived of her dear little companion, and tried to find all sorts of remedies rather than part with Heidi. But her father was firm. He did, however, promise to take Klara to Switzerland the following summer, if she were then well enough to travel and if she would be quiet and reasonable now. With a sigh, Klara resigned herself to the inevitable, begging only that Heidi's trunk be brought to her room, and packed there so that she could put into it anything she pleased, or anything that she thought might please her little friend. To this her father heartily agreed.

Meanwhile Aunt Dete arrived with Sebastian, and was left in great suspense in the antechamber. Surely, her being summoned at this hour must indicate that something unusual was going on? Mr. Sesemann went out to explain why it was necessary to send her niece immediately back to her grandfather, and Dete to accompany her that very day.

Much disappointed by this unexpected turn of events,

Dete did not hide her feelings. She remembered too well the stormy parting from the Alm-Uncle, and his warning to her never to show her face to him again. Now it seemed scarcely prudent to return with Heidi, having brought the child to him so unceremoniously before and taken her away against his will. Dete made up her mind promptly.

Today it was impossible for her to make the journey; and it was not to be thought of for tomorrow. The day after she simply could not get away at all, and, as a matter of fact, she had no idea when she might be free to do so.

Mr. Sesemann saw through her excuses and dismissed Dete without further comment. Sending for Sebastian, he ordered him to prepare for a journey. He was to take Heidi to Basle that very day, and continued home with her on the day after, and then return to Frankfurt at once. A letter to Heidi's grandfather would be given to him to explain everything.

One thing Sebastian was not to forget, Mr. Sesemann continued. "I am well known at the hotel at Basle, and the directions written on this card will provide for a good room for the little Swiss. You are then to go to her room at once and close and fasten carefully all the windows, so that they cannot be opened. The door, also, must be locked and fastened from the outside, once the child retires for the night, because she walks in her sleep and might be in great danger in a strange house if she chanced to get out of her room, and tried to open the house door. Do you understand, Sebastian?"

"Ah! So that was it!" cried Sebastian, as if a great light had suddenly illuminated the ghost.

"Yes, that was it, and here is a simpleton, too, who can tell John that he also is a coward – as much as the whole ridiculous household." And in a high state of irritation, Mr. Sesemann strode off to his own room to write the letter to the Alm-Uncle.

By this time, Heidi was in her Sunday frock, but had no idea of what was to happen.

Breakfast was already served when Mr. Sesemann walked into the dining-room saying. "Where is the child?" as he folded his finished letter and slipped it into an envelope.

Heidi appeared promptly, and went towards him to say good morning.

"Well now, and what have you to say about it all, little one?" he asked, examining her face closely.

Puzzled, Heidi looked up at him.

"You really know nothing about it, do you?" he continued, smiling. "Today you are going home! Almost at once, in fact!"

"Home!" the child turned perfectly white. She could scarcely breathe, for her heart seemed to be standing still.

"Don't you want to know more about it?"

"Oh, yes, indeed!" she replied, a high colour flooding her thin little face.

"That's better," said Mr. Sesemann, waving her to a seat at the table. "Eat a hearty breakfast, then into the carriage and away," he said encouragingly.

Heidi tried to eat, but such turmoil was taking place within her that she did not know whether she was awake or asleep. She half dreaded to find herself in her nightgown on the doorstep.

"Tell Sebastian to take a substantial lunch with him," said Mr. Sesemann to Miss Rottenmeier who entered at this moment. "The child cannot eat, which is not surprising, of course. Go into Klara's room, little one, and stay with her until the carriage comes," he added in a kindly voice, turning to Heidi.

That was exactly what Heidi was longing to do, so away she ran at once. A huge trunk stood in the middle of Klara's room with the lid still open.

"Heidi! Come here, and see what I have packed for you," Klara exclaimed, beckoning to her friend eagerly. There was a great quantity of things, dresses and aprons, handkerchiefs and sewing things, and – greatest treasure of all for the little Swiss – a basket of twelve beautiful white round rolls for the grandmother in Dorfli. In their delight over these gifts the girls forgot the coming separation, until a call from the other room reminded them.

"The carriage is ready," shouted Mr. Sesemann, and now there was no time to grieve over the parting.

Heidi flung her arms round Klara and kissed her, and then rushed into her own room for the beautiful book given her by the grandmamma, which she kept under her pillow at night. Then she opened the wardrobe wide for another precious thing which must go home with her. There it was; the old red shawl, which Miss Rottenmeier had considered too shabby to be packed in the trunk. Heidi wrapped it round her other treasure, and placed it carefully on top of the basket of rolls, where the red parcel was very conspicuous. Then she donned her pretty new hat, and left the room.

The goodbyes were quickly said, for Mr. Sesemann was waiting to put Heidi into the carriage, and Miss Rottenmeier was at the head of the stairs to take leave of her. But when the housekeeper caught sight of the shabby red shawl, she snatched the bundle from the top of the roll basket, and tossed it on the floor.

"Adelheid," she said reproachfully, "you must not leave this house carrying away anything like that! Now, goodbye."

Heidi did not dare to take back her little bundle, but she looked up at the master of the house so beseechingly, that he said at once, "Miss Rottenmeier, the child shall take home with her whatever she wishes."

Quickly Heidi retrieved her treasure.

At the carriage door, Mr. Sesemann took leave of his little Swiss, holding her small hand warmly, and wishing her a good journey. "Do not forget your friends in Frankfurt," he told her.

And for her part, Heidi thanked him bravely for all the kindness he had shown her, adding earnestly, "And the good doctor, please give him a thousand thanks for me."

Her conversation with him on the night before was fresh in her memory, as well as the good man's words. "Tomorrow everything will be all right." This was tomorrow, and everything was, and the child felt sure the doctor had something to do with it.

Then the child was lifted into the carriage, and after her came the basket, the well-stocked lunch bag, and Sebastian. "A happy journey," cried Mr. Sesemann, and they rolled away towards the railway.

All the time they were on the train, Heidi kept her basket close beside her, for the precious rolls for the grandmother were there, and she must guard them carefully. It was only now that she began to believe that she was truly on her way to the Alm, to her grandfather, to goat-Peter, and her thoughts were busy with remembering her beloved home and friends.

After a while, sleep overcame the weary child, for with all the events of the previous night and the early awakening that morning, she was exhausted. She slept until Sebastian roused her, saying urgently, "Wake up! wake up! We are in Basle."

With a night's rest, their journey was resumed, Heidi always holding the basket, which she would not give up even for a moment. At last, the train conductor cried out "Mayenfeld!" Heidi and Sebastian sprang up hastily. They were on the platform, the basket safe, and the train puffing away in the distance almost before they knew it.

Sebastian looked after it longingly, for he much preferred travel by rail than on foot, as they must now go, ending their journey with a climb up a mountain. And that, simple Sebastian was convinced, in a half-wild country full of dangers on every side.

Having looked about him cautiously, Sebastian determined to find out the safest way to Dorfli. Not far from the station he saw a cart and horse. A broad-shouldered man was lifting sacks of flour into the cart. Sebastian questioned him.

"All ways are safe here," replied the man gruffly.

Sebastian then asked the fellow how a trunk could be taken to Dorfli. The man measured the trunk with his eye, and said that if it were not too heavy he would take it to Dorfli, since he was going there. And from that, the pair at last reached the understanding that the child and her trunk should be put into the cart, and taken to Dorfli. From there Heidi could be sent up the Alm that evening.

"I can go up myself, I know the way," Heidi volunteered.

A great load fell from Sebastian's heart, as he found himself released from the necessity of climbing up the mountain. He beckoned Heidi aside and gave her a small but heavy parcel, and a letter for her grandfather. The parcel contained a present from Mr. Sesemann, he told her, and it must be looked after carefully, as his master would be very angry if it were lost.

Heidi promptly put it into the basket under the rolls, as there it would be safest. "I will not lose it," she assured Sebastian earnestly.

So Heidi, her trunk, and her basket, were hoisted into the cart with Sebastian making all the ado possible, to quiet his conscience for not going with the child himself, as he had been instructed.

At last the driver climbed up to his high seat beside Heidi, and they rolled off toward Dorfli, while the servant settled down to await the train back to Frankfurt.

The man in the cart was the baker from Dorfli. He did not know Heidi, but he knew her story well. Also he had known her parents, and felt sure at once that the much-talked-about Heidi was now in his care, although the child's name had never been mentioned in the transaction at the station. He wondered why the child was coming back, and as they jogged along he began to question her.

"You must be the little girl who lived with the Alm-Uncle," he said.

"Yes," Heidi admitted.

"Have you had a bad time of it, that you are coming back again?"

"No, I was very well off in Frankfurt."

"Why, then, are you coming home?" the baker asked.

"Only because Mr. Sesemann allowed it."

"Well, why didn't you stay there even if he did give you leave to go?"

"Because I would a thousand times rather be with my grandfather on the Alm than anywhere else in the whole world." Heidi spoke so passionately that the man stared at her, quite amazed.

"You may think differently when you get up there now," the baker muttered under his breath. "She cannot have heard how it is up there now," he added.

He began to whistle, and said no more. Looking about her, Heidi began to tremble with excitement, for she recognized the trees on the roadside, and above she could see the great jagged peaks which looked down on her, seeming to greet her like an old friend. With every turn of the wheels, her excitement increased until it seemed as if she must spring from the cart, and run without stopping to the very top. She controlled herself, however, and as it struck five, they drove into Dorfli.

At once they were surrounded by a crowd of women and children, and several men came forward to help with the child's trunk. Everyone wanted to know where she came from, and where she was going.

When the baker had lifted Heidi down, she said quickly, "My grandfather will soon come for the trunk, and I thank you for the ride," and wanted to run on. But she was delayed on every side, with everyone firing questions at her. Her face became so anxious, that at last the villagers allowed her to go on her way.

But to each other they said, "See how frightened the child is, and she has cause enough to be." Then they all began to gossip – how for the past year the Alm-Uncle had grown more and more ill-humoured, and now would not speak a word to anyone, but looked as if he would like to kill whoever crossed his path. If this poor child had any other place in the world to go, she would certainly not run into that old dragon's lair.

The baker, however, said importantly that of course he knew more about it than anyone else. And then he related how a gentleman had brought the child to Mayenfeld, had taken leave of her very affectionately and had also given him the price of the ride, plus something over, without even bargaining. Above all, *he* could truly say that Heidi had been happy in Frankfurt, and yet had come back of her own accord to live with her grandfather.

This surprising news flashed through the village. In every house they soon were talking of how Heidi had left all sorts of comforts behind her, and had returned of her own accord to her grandfather.

Heidi had all this time been climbing the mountain as fast as she could, but often she was obliged to stand still, for she was continually out of breath. The heavy basket on her arm grew heavier as the climb grew steeper, but she pressed on. The soft white rolls must be delivered to the grandmother – and as soon as possible, too.

When at last she spied goat-Peter's cottage in the hollow on the Alm-side, her heart began to beat wildly. At last she pushed the door open and sprang into the little room, standing there, utterly breathless, unable to say a word.

"Ah," said a voice from the corner, "that is the way the child Heidi used to come running in to see me! If I could once more in my life have her with me! Who is it that has come in?"

"It is I, Grandmother – Heidi," cried the child, and rushed towards the old woman. Falling to her knees she seized the grandmother's hand, and laid her head upon the old woman's lap, not able to speak a word in her happiness.

At first the grandmother could not speak, either, but then she began stroking the child's curly hair, repeating over and over, "Yes, it is the dear child's hair, and her voice. Oh, the dear God has been good to me!" and happy tears streamed from her old eyes. "Is it really you, child? I can scarcely believe it."

"Yes, really, Grandmother," Heidi said reassuringly. "Please don't cry any more. Here I am, and will come every day to you, and never, never go away again. And here, Grandmother, now you won't have to eat hard bread for many days!" Heidi took the rolls from the basket, and counted them one after another into the old woman's lap, until it was full.

"Child, child! what a blessing you bring with you!" cried the grandmother. "But the greatest blessing of all is yourself."

Peter's mother entered at this moment, and stood quite still in amazement. Then she cried out, "It is Heidi! Can I believe my eyes?"

Heidi jumped up to shake hands with Brigitte, who could not admire the child enough, and walked round and round her saying, "Oh, mother, if you could only see the beautiful dress Heidi is wearing! One can scarcely recognize her! And the hat with the feather, on the table! Put it on, Heidi, I want to see how you look in it."

"No, I don't want it," said the child. "You may have it. I shall not wear it again for I have my old one which I like much better." So saying, she opened the red shawl bundle, and took out the hat, more crumpled than ever from the journey. Heidi did not care about that, for she had never forgotten how her grandfather had declared, when she left the Alm, that he would never look upon her in a hat with feathers. Therefore she had always kept the old hat, hoping to wear it when she returned home.

Brigitte, however, said she could not take it, but it might be sold to the daughter of the teacher in Dorfli for a good sum of money, if Heidi really did not want it. Heidi only shook her head, and put the hat in the corner behind the grandmother. Then taking off her pretty city frock, she wrapped the old red shawl over her little undershirt with its short sleeves, and felt she was now ready for the Alm.

Taking the grandmother's hand, she said, "Now I must go to my grandfather, but I will come back tomorrow to see you. Goodnight."

"You will surely come again, little one." The old woman held the small hand tightly in hers, and could hardly let the child go from her.

"Why have you taken off your pretty dress?" Brigitte asked.

"I would prefer to go up to my grandfather without it, because he might not know me. You said that you hardly knew me in it."

"Oh. *He* would have known you. But do be careful, for Peterkin says that the Alm-Uncle is cross all the time now, and never speaks a pleasant word."

"Goodnight," was all the answer Heidi gave, as she resumed her climb up the Alm with her bundle on her arm. The evening sun lighted the green slopes, and, up above, the great snow field gleamed in the distance.

Every few steps Heidi had to stop and turn about, for the highest peak lay behind her. The red glow of sunset fell on the grass at her feet. Everything was even more beautiful than she had remembered. The pinnacles flamed up to heaven, the white snow field glowed, and rosy-red clouds drifted across the sky. Heidi stood in all this beauty, and happy tears rolled down her cheeks. Folding her hands she looked up to heaven, giving thanks to the good God who had brought her home again.

Not until the light about her began to fade, could Heidi tear herself away from the spot. Then she began to hurry up the mountain at such a pace that before long she saw the tops of the three pine trees, the hut itself, and at last, on the bench, her grandfather, smoking his pipe. Heidi broke into a run, and before her grandfather rightly knew who was before him, the child had thrown her arms round his neck, clasping him tightly and repeating over and over, in her happiness, "Grandfather, Grandfather, Grandfather!"

The old man could not say a word, his eyes moist with tears. Loosening Heidi's arms from about his neck, he put her on his knees and inspected her steadily. "So you have come home again, Heidi," he said. "How is this? You don't look very fine." He touched the old red shawl, and the white slip. "Have they sent you away?"

"Oh no, Grandfather," Heidi said eagerly. "You must not think that. They were all kind to me – Klara and Grandmamma and Mr. Sesemann. But you see, Grandfather, I couldn't bear it any longer. I had to come home to you. Often I thought I should smother in Frankfurt, and I felt so wretched, but I didn't say anything because it would have been ungrateful. And then, suddenly one morning Mr. Sesemann called me very early – but I think it was because of what the doctor said – perhaps it is all written in the letter!" Heidi jumped down from his knees to pull the letter and the parcel out of the basket, which she had dropped on the ground by the bench, and she gave both to her grandfather.

"This is yours," he said, putting the heavy package beside her on the bench. "It is a great deal of money to have on the Alm." He read the letter in silence, and then thrust it into his pocket. "Do you feel you could drink a little milk with me, Heidi?" he asked, taking the child's hand in his. "But carry your money with you. It can buy you a new bed, and clothes enough for many years."

"I don't want money, Grandfather, and I have a bed, you know. And Klara has given me so many clothes that I shall never have to buy any for years, and years, and years, I'm sure."

"Take the money, nevertheless, and store it in the cupboard. You may want it some day."

Heidi picked up the parcel because he wished it, and danced into the hut behind her grandfather. There she was soon peeping into all the corners, delighted to be home once more. Presently she climbed up into the loft, and from there exclaimed, "Oh, Grandfather, my bed has gone!"

"We'll soon put it back again. I didn't know you were coming back," he answered huskily. "Come down for your milk, now."

The little girl clambered down, seated herself on her high stool in her old place, seized her mug, and drank so hungrily that her grandfather saw she had not lost her old tastes. "There is no milk in the whole wide world so good as ours, Grandfather," she told him with a deep sigh of satisfaction.

A shrill, well-remembered whistle sounded outside. Lightning-quick, Heidi sprang through the door. Down from the heights came the little army of goats, with Peter in their midst. He saw her and stood still as if rooted to the spot, staring at Heidi in speechless surprise.

"Good evening, Peter," she called out, and rushed in among the goats. "Schwänli! Bärli! Do you remember me?"

The animals showed soon enough that they recognized her voice, for they rubbed their heads against her and began to bleat with joy. One after another Heidi called them all by name, and they all ran to her at once. The impatient Thistlebird jumped over two other goats to get near, while Snowball, forgetting her timidity, pushed aside the big bold Turk, who stood in her way.

Heidi put her arm about gentle little Snowball, stroking her again and again, and patted the restless Thistlebird, and was pushed and butted affectionately, nearer and nearer to Peter, who had never stirred from the time he saw her.

"Come down here, Peter, and speak to me," Heidi said to him at last.

"You here again!" he blurted, recovering his speech, and looking very glad – for Peter. Then, as if it had been only yesterday, he repeated the old question, that he had so often asked in the evening when they came down from the pasture together, "Will you go with me again tomorrow?"

"No, not tomorrow. Perhaps the day after. Tomorrow I must go down to visit your grandmother."

"It's a good thing you've come back," said Peter, in great satisfaction, as he started to go home.

But it was harder than ever before to get the flock away, for as soon as he had collected them about him, and Heidi began moving towards the shed with one arm around Schwänli's and the other around Bärli's neck, then they all turned and ran back to her. At last she went into the shed, out of sight with her two goats, and closed the door, or Peter might never have got his flock down the mountain that night.

Returning into the hut, Heidi found her bed again arranged in the loft. It was high and fragrant, for the hay was quite fresh, with the great white linen sheet spread carefully over it, and tucked firmly under. Heidi lay down and was asleep in an instant. And she slept as she had not slept for an entire year.

At least ten times during that night her grandfather left his bed, and climbed the ladder to see if she slept quietly, or if she showed any sign of the night-wandering mentioned in the letter from Mr. Sesemann. But there was no danger of that now for the child. Her ardent longing had been stilled. She slept without stirring, for she had seen the mountains and the pinnacles glow in the night and the setting sun, and she had heard the murmuring pines, and she was at home on the Alm.

Chapter 14

WHEN THE CHURCH BELLS RING

HEIDI stood under the swaying pines, waiting for her grandfather, who was going to collect her trunk from Dorfli, while she visited the grandmother. The child could hardly wait to see the grandmother again to find out how the rolls had tasted.

Her grandfather came out of the hut at last, looked about him with satisfaction, and said, "Now we can go down."

The day was Saturday, and the Alm-Uncle's custom had always been to put everything to rights about the place. This morning he had begun work early, and he had a right to look about him with contentment now, for by early afternoon everything was fresh and clean.

They parted at goat-Peter's cottage, and Heidi darted in. As always, she was received with a joyous welcome.

The blind woman grasped the child's hand, holding on tightly, as if she feared that her treasure might again be torn from her. The rolls were delicious, she told the child, and had so strengthened her that the grandmother declared herself quite another person. Brigitte added, that for fear they would be gone too soon, her mother had eaten only a single roll. If with her old teeth she could munch one every day, it might really benefit her health.

Heidi thought this over, and at last hit upon a plan.

"I know what I can do! I can write to Klara, and ask her to send me as many more rolls, for I had collected a great heap in my wardrobe, and when they were taken away, Klara promised to give me as many more. And she will, I'm sure."

"Oh, that is a fine idea," Brigitte said, "But I'm afraid they would get very hard. If only now and then we could have a fresh batch! The baker in Dorfli makes them, but I can only manage to buy black bread."

Now Heidi's eyes sparkled. "I have a wonderful lot of money, Grandmother!" she exclaimed in triumph. "Now I know what to do with it. Every single day you shall have a fresh roll, and on Sunday, two. Peter will bring them from Dorfli." Heidi fairly danced in her delight at the prospect.

"No, child, no! that we can't allow. The money was not given to you for that. Your grandfather will tell you what use to make of it."

But Heidi would not listen to any such talk. Instead, she danced about, and shouted "Yes, Grandmother, you shall have a fresh roll every day, and get really strong. Perhaps then," she added, "it will be light for you again. Perhaps it is dark only because you are so weak."

The good old woman smiled silently, for she would not spoil the child's happiness. But as Heidi went capering about the room, she saw the old hymnbook, and with it a new idea came to her. "Grandmother," she said, "I have learned to read quite well. Shall I read you something from the old hymnbook?"

"Oh, Heidi! can you really read? Oh what a blessing!" the old woman exclaimed.

Heidi climbed on a chair and brought down the book from the shelf. Seated on her footstool beside the old woman, she asked simply, "What shall I read?"

"Whatever you please, child," the grandmother said, her voice trembling with expectation.

Heidi leafed through the pages, scanning the lines. At last she said, "Here, I have found a beautiful psalm. Listen, Grandmother:

'The Lord is my shepherd; I shall not want.

He maketh me to lie down in green pastures. . .' " She read in a sweet, clear voice, and the grandmother leaned towards her, scarcely breathing, blissful happiness upon her lined face, while tears coursed down her cheeks.

"Once more, dear child, once more," she begged, each time Heidi stopped reading – and Heidi read on and on.

At long last the old woman sat back in her chair with a deep, heartfelt sigh. "Oh, Heidi, your reading makes it light for me, my child. Light in my heart. You will never know the good you have done me."

Heidi beamed with pleasure, for never had she seen the grandmother so content, and so at peace.

Someone knocked upon the window, and it was the Alm-Uncle, there to take his granddaughter back up the Alm with him.

Heidi went to him quickly, but not without assuring her blind friend that she would come again tomorrow. Even if she went with Peter to the pasture, she would come back in the afternoon, she said, and left the old woman nodding happily.

Brigitte followed Heidi to the door with the dress and hat Heidi had left behind the day before, begging the child to take her things home with her. The dress she did take, for as grandfather had already recognized her, there was nothing to fear on that score. But the hat she refused even to touch. Brigitte could keep it, for Heidi would never, never again put it on her head.

Going up the Alm, Heidi recounted to her grandfather all that had happened in the cottage, about the rolls that could be bought in Dorfli, and about her reading. Then she returned to the rolls again, saying, "Even if Grandmother will not take it, you will give the money to me, won't you? Then I can give some to Peter every morning to buy a fresh roll with, and on Sunday, two."

"But the bed, Heidi," reminded the Alm-Uncle. "A real bed would be a fine thing for you, and there would still be money for a great many rolls."

The child, however, gave him no peace, insisting that she slept far better on her bed of hay then she ever did in Frankfurt on a bed of down. She begged so earnestly, that at last he said, "It is your own money, child. Do with it

116

what you will. You can buy rolls for the grandmother for many years, if you wish."

"Good!" shouted Heidi. "Now she won't need to eat the hard black bread! Oh, Grandfather, now everything is fine, and it never was so beautiful before, never, since we were born!" and she danced along beside her grandfather, singing happily.

All at once she paused and grew thoughtful. "If the good God had granted my prayer at once," she said, "when I begged him so hard, then I should have come home long ago, and brought Grandmother only a few rolls. I could not have read to her. God arranged everything far better than I could have done. It has all come true, just as the grandmamma told me it would. Now I shall always pray as the grandmamma told me to do, thanking Him. For even if what I've asked is not granted, I shall remember how it was in Frankfurt, and that He is planning something much better. We'll pray together, Grandfather. We'll not forget Him, and then the good God will not forget us."

"And if anyone should forget to pray?" the old man asked softly.

"Oh, then things will not go well for him. The Lord will let him go his own way, and if he complains, nobody will pity him. They will all say that he went from the Lord first, and now God will not help him."

"That is true, Heidi, but how did you find it out?"

"Grandmamma explained it all to me," Heidi said solemnly.

They walked on for a while in silence, and then her grandfather said, as if thinking out loud, "When this is once so, it remains so. There is no going back. If God has forgotten a man, he is forgotten forever more."

"Oh, no, Grandfather! One can go back! The grandmamma told me a beautiful story about it from a book she gave me. I haven't shown it to you yet, but we are almost home, and I will get it for you right away. You will soon see what a beautiful story this is and how true."

The child rushed into the hut to find her precious book, while the grandfather set down from his back the basket in which he had brought half of Heidi's things up the Alm. The trunkful would have been too heavy for him. Then he sat down thoughtfully on the bench.

Heidi came running out again quickly, the big book in her hands. She settled herself beside the old man and the precious book opened itself at the right place.

In her own earnest way, Heidi read of the Prodigal Son: how he had demanded his property of his father and then gone off and squandered it all. When he had nothing left, he'd become a servant, ill-treated, starved, and in rags. How he wept for homesickness, and at last resolved to go back to his father and to beg his forgiveness.

" 'Even though I am not worthy to be called your son, perhaps you will let me be as one of your servants,' " Heidi read compassionately.

But when he came near his father's house, and his father saw him, she went on, the old man came running to meet his son.

"And what do you think, Grandfather?" Heidi asked. "Do you think the father was angry and sent him away with cruel words? Listen: 'And the father saw him and pitied him, and ran and fell on his neck, and kissed him. And the son said, I have sinned before heaven and in thy sight, and am no more worthy to be called thy son. But the father said to his servants: Bring the best dress, and put it on him; and put a ring on his hand, and shoes on his feet; and bring the fatted calf, and kill it, and let us eat, and be merry: for this my son was dead, and is alive again; he was lost, and is found. And they began to be merry.' " Heidi stopped reading and looked full at the grandfather.

"Isn't that a beautiful story?" she asked, and then felt sadly disappointed, for the old man sat silently beside her and did not appear at all pleased, as she had expected.

"Yes, the story is beautiful," he said at last, but heavily, and with his face so serious, that Heidi turned to her pictures. Presently she held her book before her grandfather, saying, "See, how happy he is!" and pointed to the picture of the prodigal, restored to his father.

Hours later, when Heidi had long been asleep, her grandfather climbed the little ladder to the hayloft and placed his lamp near Heidi's bed, so that the light shone on her. She lay with folded hands, for Heidi had not forgotten to pray. On her face was an expression of peace and trust, and her grandfather stood a long time, looking at her.

At last he, too, folded his hands, fell to his knees, and with bowed head, murmured, "Father, I have sinned against heaven and in Thy sight, and am no more worthy to be called Thy son," and as he said this, great tears rolled down his cheeks.

At dawn the old man stood before his hut, and looked about him with a new sparkle in his eyes. The sunlight of this beautiful Sunday morning flooded over mountain and valley. From far below came sounds of early church bells and in the pines the birds were already at their happy songs.

The old man stepped back into the hut, calling to Heidi, "Come, little one, the sun is up. Put on your Sunday frock, and we'll go to church together."

Heidi jumped up at once. This was a new call from the grandfather and one to be followed without delay. It took her but a few minutes to come running down in her pretty Frankfurt dress. At the sight of her grandfather, she stood spellbound, for there he was dressed in a coat with silver buttons, which she had never seen before. "Why, Grandfather," she exclaimed, "how splendid you are in your Sunday coat!"

The old man looked pleased and smiled at the child as he said, "And you also in yours. Quite elegant. But come now." He took Heidi's hand in his, and they walked down the mountain together. On every side the sound of the clear church bells came towards them, growing fuller and richer as they drew closer to Dorfli.

Heidi listened, entranced, "Oh, Grandfather, it's like a great festival," she breathed.

In Dorfli all the people were already gathered in the church, and the singing had begun, when Heidi and the Alm-Uncle entered together. They took seats on the last bench behind all the others. But in the middle of the singing, the man next to them nudged his neighbour with his elbow, and whispered hoarsely, "The Alm-Uncle. The Alm-Uncle is in the church."

Soon word flew from one to another, until the church seemed to be filled with buzzing bees. "The Alm-Uncle. The Alm-Uncle."

The women kept turning round every minute, and most of them fell out in their singing, so that the leader had the greatest difficulty in keeping them together at all.

But when the pastor began his sermon, the congregation grew quiet, for there was such warmth and thanksgiving in his words that none failed to be impressed. It seemed as if a great blessing had fallen on them all.

When the service was over, the Alm-Uncle, holding his granddaughter by the hand, went out of the church to the parsonage. Everyone else looked after them, to see if he really did go into the pastor's house – which he did.

Then they gathered to gossip excitedly over the fact that he had at last appeared in the church, and they watched the door of the pastor's house, to see whether when he came out he would look angry, or seem at peace. No one could even guess what had brought the old man down from the Alm, nor what it might mean.

A change of feeling had already sprung up among a few of the villagers, and one of these said to the others, "The Alm-Uncle cannot be so bad, after all. Did you not see how tenderly he held the little one by the hand?" And another said, "I always said so. Besides, he would not go to the pastor's if he were so really wicked, for he would be afraid. People stretch things so."

And the baker had to dip his oar in, too, saying, "Didn't

I tell you that, from the very first? Whoever heard of a child who had all she wanted to eat and drink and everything she could wish for, running back again to a grandfather who was harsh, and who made her afraid of him?"

Gradually they began to think more kindly of the Alm-Uncle, and the women joined in and told how much good they had heard of the old man from goat-Peterkin and his grandmother. This placed the Alm-Uncle in a better light than ever, until at last all the villagers began to believe that they were waiting there before the parsonage to welcome back an old friend, whom they had long missed.

In the meanwhile the Alm-Uncle had knocked on the door of the study, and the pastor had opened it and admitted the visitors at once, not seeming at all surprised, but rather as if he had been expecting them. He seized the hand of the old man, and shook it heartily, as the Alm-Uncle stood there, unable to speak at first and unprepared for such a kind reception.

At last collecting himself, he said, "I came to beg the pastor to forget what I told him on the Alm, hoping that he will not hold it against me, that I was so obstinate concerning his well-meant advice. You were perfectly right, Pastor, and I was wrong, and I will now follow your advice, and find a lodging for myself for the coming winter in Dörfli. The winter months are too severe for this little one up there. She is too delicate, and even if the folk down here do look a bit askance at me, I deserve it, and if the pastor will stand by me, I will make out, I'm sure."

The kindly pastor beamed as he took the old man's hand and pressed it, much moved. "Neighbour," he said, "you have been to the right church before you came down to mine. And, if you will come to live amongst us again, you shall not regret it, but always find in me a true friend and a warm welcome. I shall look forward to many pleasant evenings in your company, for it was most agreeable in the past and shall be in the future, I am certain. We shall also find some good friends for your little grandchild."

So saying, the pastor touched Heidi's curly head, and taking her by the hand led her out as he accompanied the grandfather. He took leave of the pair outside the door, so all the people standing about could see how he held the Alm-Uncle's hand, and kept shaking it, as if the old man were his dearest friend.

Scarcely had the door closed behind the pastor, than all the villagers crowded round the Alm-Uncle, each one wishing to be first. So many hands were stretched out that he did not know which one to take. One said, "I am glad, Uncle, that you have come amongst us again." Another, "I have long wanted to speak with you again." And so it went on, from all sides, and when he told them that he thought of coming down to live amongst them in the winter, there was so much ado that it really warmed the old man's heart and reassured him of his welcome.

Even when they left Dorfli, many of the villagers accompanied the grandfather and the child part way up the Alm, and many begged him, at parting, to call at their homes when he next came down their way. When at last the people had turned back down the mountain, the old man watched them with such a glow on his face that it seemed as if the sun itself was shining within him.

Heidi looked at him lovingly and said, "Grandfather, today you are more handsome than you ever were before."

"Do you think so, Heidi?" he said, and laughed happily. "Yes, today all is well with me, more so than I deserve. The good God meant this to be when he sent you to the Alm, Heidi."

When they reached goat-Peter's cottage, the grandfather opened the door and entered. "God bless you, Grandmother!" he cried. "Shall we go to the quilting together, before the autumn winds blow?"

"Oh, heaven! That is the Alm-Uncle, indeed!" cried the old woman in delight. "That I should have liked to see this day! Now I can thank you for all that you have done for us. May God reward you!" Pressing the hand of her old friend, she continued, "I have but one request to make of you, Uncle, do not let Heidi go away ever again. You do not know what she means to me!" and she reached out to hold the child fast, for Heidi had already nestled into her accustomed place.

"Never fear, Grandmother," replied the Uncle soothingly, "Heidi shall never leave either of us again."

Then Brigitte drew the Uncle away into a corner and showed him the pretty hat and feather, as she told him its little story. Of course, she said, she would not take such a thing from a child.

The grandfather looked approvingly at his Heidi. "The hat is hers," he said, "and if she chooses not to put it on again, that is all right. And if she has given it to you, keep it."

Brigitte was delighted. "It is a lovely hat," she said. "Just look at it!" and she held it high above her head. "Think what wonderful things the child has brought back from Frankfurt! I have been wondering if I should send my Peterkin there, also. What do you think, Uncle?"

His eyes twinkling, the Uncle declared that it could do Peter no harm, but it would be best to wait for a good opportunity.

At that moment, Peter came in at the door, but only after he had almost broken his head on it, for in his haste he had run into it full tilt. But something unheard of had occurred. A letter with Heidi's name on it had been given him by the postmaster in Dorfli to deliver. Now Peter held it out stiffly towards her.

The letter was from Klara Sesemann, Heidi saw at once. Everyone sat around the table while Heidi read it aloud.

It told how Klara had found the hours very dull since Heidi left her, and that she had begged her father so hard to take her to Ragatzbad, that he had at last promised to do so in the coming autumn. Her grandmamma would come, too, for she wished to visit Heidi and her grandfather on the Alm. Moreover, Grandmamma sent Heidi a message:

that it was quite right for her to wish to bring the rolls to the blind grandmother. And, lest they should be too dry, she must have some coffee to moisten them, and therefore some was already on the way. Also, she hoped to visit the grandmother herself when she came to Dörfli.

Now came the questions and the wonderings, and everyone was so excited, that even the Alm-Uncle did not notice how late it had grown. At last the grandmother said, "The best of all is when an old friend comes and gives you his hand again, just as he did long ago. In that is blessed comfort. You will come again soon, Uncle, and bring Heidi with you?"

The Uncle promised, and shook hands gravely on it. Now, indeed, it was time to go, and Heidi and her grandfather climbed up the Alm together. The sweet clear music of the bells which had called them in the morning in the valley, now seemed to float about them again as they returned to their dear mountain home, which lay so peacefully in the warm golden evening light.

Her home, her mountains, thought Heidi happily. Forever and forever and forever.

PART II

Heidi Uses What She Learned

Chapter 15

A JOURNEY

ONE SUNNY afternoon in September, kindly old Dr. Classen, who had decided so wisely that Heidi should be sent back to her grandfather, was walking slowly through the wide streets of Frankfurt towards Mr. Sesemann's house. The day was bright and beautiful, but the doctor scarcely noticed, for his eyes were fixed upon the stones at his feet, and on his face there was an expression of deep sadness. Early that spring, the good doctor had lost his only daughter, a lovely girl, who since her mother's death had been the joy of his life.

Sebastian admitted the doctor with respectful sympathy, and Mr. Sesemann came forward at once to greet his friend.

"I am so glad that you have come," Mr. Sesemann said, grasping the doctor's hand. "I must talk to you once more concerning Klara. To me she seems much better, and I cannot agree with your last decision."

"My dear Sesemann," the doctor sighed as he seated himself. "I do wish that your mother were here. She sees things so clearly; but with you there is no reasoning possible, it seems. This is the third time you have sent for me, although I keep telling you the same thing each time."

"I know, and it must seem very foolish to you, doctor," Mr. Sesemann admitted, "but surely you can understand how hard it is for me to deprive Klara of the pleasure to which she has been looking forward so eagerly – the trip to Switzerland and the visit to Heidi. Just thinking about it has made her happy for so many long days and months. I cannot deprive her of this joy."

"Yet you must, Sesemann," the doctor said, very decidedly. "Consider it rationally, my friend. Klara has not had such a bad summer as this one for many years. It would be madness, therefore, to undertake a long journey with her in this poor condition. It is September now, and although it may still be pleasant on the Alm, the days are growing short, and it will soon be cold. Klara could not spend the nights on the mountain, but only a few hours of each day. The journey from Ragatzbad would require several hours, with Klara carried up the mountain in a chair.

"In short, Sesemann, the trip is impossible, but I'll go in with you and talk with Klara. She is a sensible girl, and I will tell her of a plan I have for her. In the spring she shall go to Ragatzbad, and take the baths there, until it is warm and pleasant on the mountain. Then she can be carried up from time to time, and the visits with Heidi will then refresh and strengthen her. That would not be the case now. You do understand, Sesemann, that the only hope for your child's ultimate recovery is through the most careful treatment and watchfulness, do you not?"

"Doctor, tell me truthfully, is there any hope for improvement in my daughter's condition?"

The doctor shrugged. "Very little," he said sadly. "But think, my friend, compare your position with mine. You have your child. No empty house awaits you whenever you return. Although she is an invalid, Klara can enjoy many things, surrounded as she is by every luxury and care, even though she is occasionally deprived of – well, this trip, for example. And you, Sesemann, can count yourself happy, for you are not alone. Think of my empty house."

Mr. Sesemann bowed his head, frowning, and began to pace the room with great strides. At last he stopped and tapped his good friend on the arm, saying, "Doctor, I cannot see you so depressed. You must come out of yourself a little. I have an excellent plan. *You* will go up to the Alm, to visit the little Swiss and her grandfather in our name!"

Taken completely by surprise, the doctor would have declined at once, had his friend given him the chance. But Sesemann was so delighted by this thought, that he seized the doctor's arm and rushed him into Klara's room.

Klara, who loved the doctor dearly, especially now in his sadness, held out her hands to him.

Her father went round to the other side of her chair, and began at once to talk about the trip to Switzerland which had been promised, but which Klara now must give up, because of her health. She was not equal to it at present, he said, and went on hurriedly, before the dreaded tears came, to divulge his new plan. What would she think if the doctor went up in their stead? It would be such a good change for their friend – if they could persuade him to do it. Would she help?

Klara choked down her tears, knowing how they distressed her father, but she was almost overwhelmed with disappointment. The Swiss journey, and the pleasure of seeing Heidi again, were cherished dreams which had sustained her through long hours of pain. It was hard to give them up, but she knew that her father deprived her only of necessity, and for good reason. So now she turned to the good doctor bravely.

"Please, dear Dr. Classen, will you go to Heidi?" she asked coaxingly, stroking his hand. "Go to see how they live up there on the Alm, and meet her grandfather, and Peter, and the goats, that I've heard so much about! And will you take Heidi all the presents that I had planned to carry with me! There is something for the blind grandmother, too. If you will go, dear doctor, I promise to take all the cod-liver oil you want me to, while you are away."

The good doctor smiled tenderly at the earnest little invalid. "If that is your solemn promise, I will certainly go, Klara. When shall I start?" he asked, almost laughing now.

"Tomorrow morning," she told him promptly.

"Quite right," added her father. "The weather's fine, and no time should be lost."

"Next you will be scolding me because I have not already started," the doctor teased, "so I shall go off at once."

But now Klara held him fast, for she had many messages for Heidi, and then she begged him to take note of everything in the hut, and of everything that she had heard of in her long talks with Heidi. The bundle of presents, Klara said, would be sent to the doctor's house as soon as Miss Rottenmeier returned to pack them. Just now she was out, shopping.

Dr. Classen assured his friends that he would carry out all their wishes, and as soon as he returned he would hasten to give Klara an account of all that he had seen and heard. They now parted affectionately, and already the good doctor seemed to be walking with a lighter step.

While Sebastian was conducting the doctor downstairs, Klara summoned Tinette.

"Take the box from the table by the window, Tinette, and fill it with nice fresh cakes, like the ones we have with our coffee," Klara directed, "and bring it back quickly."

The maid took the box and went off saucily, somehow guessing for whom the cakes were intended.

As the doctor hurried out of the Sesemann doorway, he saw Miss Rottenmeier returning from her shopping expedition. A strong gust of wind had caught her shawl, puffing it out on each side until she looked like a ship under full sail. The doctor drew back, startled by the apparition.

And Miss Rottenmeier, who had long cherished a profound admiration, not to say affection, for Dr. Classen, also drew back, meaning to make way for him to pass. The high wind, however, sent her on full tilt against the doctor. The housekeeper was greatly upset by this absurd situation, but the doctor quickly smoothed out her ruffled feelings, for he had a way with ladies.

Then he told her of his intended journey to Switzerland, and begged her to pack carefully the presents he was to take to little Heidi — for no one could pack so nicely and firmly as Miss Rottenmeier, he told her, with a courtly bow. And thus he left the lady, sighing happily after him.

Klara, who had been expecting less grace from the housekeeper when it came to the packing of the gifts, found her surprisingly pleasant. She cleared the table without a frown, and arranged the varied gifts upon it.

There was a long, wool cape, with a warm hood for Heidi; then came a thick, soft shawl, for the blind grandmother. Next was the great box of fresh cakes, also for the grandmother, and a huge sausage for the whole family. A bag of tobacco was for the grandfather, so fond of smoking his pipe on the bench in front of the hut. After these came a great many mysterious packages of all sizes, which Klara had prepared to surprise and please her little friend.

Finished at last with the enormous task of packing, Miss Rottenmeier stood back to admire her handiwork. Klara looked at the bundle also, her thoughts far away on the Alm, picturing the scene when Heidi opened everything. How she would jump and shout for joy. And how she, herself would have loved to see her little friend's delight at all the surprises.

Then Sebastian was called and his eyes went wide at the size of the parcel, but he swung it upon his shoulder with a smile and carried it off to the doctor's house.

Chapter 16

A GUEST ON THE ALM

A ROSY dawn glowed on the mountain peaks, and the fresh morning breeze sang in the pine trees behind the hut. Heidi heard it, and opened her eyes. It was like a voice, calling her outdoors. But first she must dress, for she knew now that one must always appear neat and orderly, and not run about like a wild creature.

When at last she came down the little hayloft ladder, her grandfather's bed was empty, so out she ran. Her grandfather stood looking at the sky, to see what the weather was to be. The rosy clouds floated high, and the sky became bluer and bluer. Up above, the pastureland was flooded with golden light as the sun climbed over the lofty peaks.

"Oh, how beautiful!" Heidi cried. "Good morning, Grandfather."

"Good morning to you, Bright Eyes," said the old man, taking her hand in his for a moment.

Then Heidi ran under the pines to listen to their windsong.

Meanwhile her grandfather had gone to the shed to milk the goats, and to wash and brush them. Then he led them out, all ready for their morning trip to the pasture. Heidi ran to the animals to caress them and speak to them gently, as always, with an arm around each. They, in turn, bleated and pressed close to her.

Peter's shrill whistle now came from below, and then the nimble Thistlebird, as usual, appeared well ahead of the flock.

"Today you can come with us again," Peter shouted to Heidi by way of salutation.

"No, I cannot, Peter. My friends may come from Frankfurt at any moment and I must be here to welcome them."

"You have said that again and again for a long time," grumbled the lad.

"And I shall keep on saying it until they do come," Heidi insisted.

"They can stay with the Uncle," Peter objected.

"What keeps the army from marching?" said the powerful voice of the old man in the hut. There was a note in his voice that Peter and his goats knew well, for off they all scrambled up the mountain without delay.

Heidi laughed and ran into the cottage. Since her stay in Frankfurt she was aware of many things in the hut that she had not noticed before. She could no longer see anything lying about, or hanging where it did not belong without doing something about it. She picked up everything that made the room look disorderly, and put it carefully into the cupboard. Then she smoothed and patted her bed in the loft, to get it into proper shape. Below, the stools and benches must be placed just so, and with a cloth she wiped and polished the table so industriously that it was quite white. Her grandfather often came in while she was at work, and observed her with a pleased air, saying, "My little one did not go away and learn nothing," or "It's always Sunday with us here, since Heidi's come back."

So today, after Peter and his army had left, and Heidi and her grandfather had breakfasted, she went straight to her housework. But it was hard to keep at it, for the day was so beautiful outside. It could not be resisted, and out she went.

The sparkling sunshine lighted up the mountain above, and flooded the valley below with its warm beauty. The grassy slope looked so soft and inviting, the child could scarcely keep from dashing over there. But Heidi remembered that the three-legged stool stood in the middle of the hut, and the table was not yet cleared from breakfast. Dutifully she went back to her work. It was no use. The music in the pines soon called her, and out she went to dance to the enchanting tune.

Her grandfather, too, left his work to see his little girl gambolling under the old trees. He watched her a while, laughing softly before he turned to go back into the shed.

All at once she called, "Grandfather, come back! come back!"

As he whirled, fearful lest she had hurt herself, he saw her dashing down the slope, calling out excitedly, "They're coming, they're coming! and the doctor's coming first of all!"

Heidi rushed to her old friend, and he reached out and caught her in his arms. "Thank you, thank you, thank you a thousand times!" she exclaimed.

"Bless you, Heidi," he answered. "But what are you thanking me for?"

"For letting me come home again to my grandfather," the little girl said simply.

The doctor's face lighted with pleasure. Weighted down by his burden of sorrow, he had climbed the mountain, absorbed in his own sad thoughts, paying no heed to the beauty around him. He had scarcely expected so hearty a greeting from the little girl whom he had seen but seldom in Frankfurt. The fact that he came only to bring her disappointment had him expecting no welcome at all. But here he was, held fast by Heidi, and lovingly, at that.

"Come now," he said at last, "take me to your grandfather, and show me where you live."

"But where are Klara and Grandmamma?" Heidi asked.

"Ah, Heidi, I have come alone. Klara was not strong enough to travel, and so her grandmamma did not come either. But in the springtime when the days are warm and long, then they will surely come."

Poor little Heidi was stunned with disappointment. The doctor watched her silently. There was no sound save for the sighing of the wind in the trees.

Then Heidi suddenly remembered why she had run down

the hill so gladly. The good doctor was here! and she looked up at him, quickly, surprising such a look of sorrow in his eyes that she was startled.

She could not bear to see anyone sad without suffering also, and dear Dr. Classen, least of all. He must be feeling disappointed because Klara and Grandmamma could not come with him, Heidi decided, and she set about at once to console him.

"It will not be so very long before the spring," she said. "The time will pass quickly, and when they come, they can stay much longer, and Klara will like that better, I'm sure. And now we will go to my grandfather."

Hand in hand they climbed uphill, to the cottage, with Heidi so anxious to cheer the doctor, that in the end she believed everything she'd said herself, and was almost consoled. When they reached her grandfather she was able to call out quite cheerfully "They are not here now, but it will not be long before they come."

Dr. Classen was no stranger to the Alm-Uncle, for Heidi had spoken of him often. Now the old man shook hands with his guest, and gave him a hearty welcome. The two men sat down on the bench, and the doctor made room for Heidi by his side. Then he told them how Mr. Sesemann had urged him to undertake the journey, and leaning down towards Heidi, he said something would soon come up the mountain that had travelled with him from Frankfurt. "And that something's arrival will give you much more pleasure than could the old doctor's," he added mysteriously.

Heidi could hardly wait, then, to find out what it was.

The Alm-Uncle invited the doctor to come up every day and stay on the Alm as long as he wished. He could not ask him to pass the night there, as the hut had no proper accommodation for such a guest, but he suggested that, instead of going all the way back to Ragatz, the doctor try the inn at Dörfli, which he would find simple but clean and well-kept. To this the doctor readily agreed.

It was midday now. The wind had ceased, and the old pines were silent. The Alm-Uncle brought out the table from the hut. "Now Heidi," he directed, "bring out what we need for dinner. Our fare is simple, but our dining room is grand."

"Indeed, it is," the doctor agreed, gazing down into the sunlit valley, and added with some surprise, "And I am famished."

Heidi ran back and forth, bringing out everything that she could from the cupboard, delighted to be able to serve the doctor. Her grandfather soon appeared from the hut, with a steaming jug of milk and toasted golden cheese. Then he cut thin, delicious slices of the rosy meat, prepared and dried in the pure mountain air. Their guest ate and drank heartily, declaring that nothing had tasted so good as this to him for a whole year.

"Indeed, our Klara must come up here," he said enthusiastically. "She would gather new strength; and if she eats as I have done today, she will soon grow too plump for her clothes and be sounder than she has ever been in all her life."

As they sat, talking, a man toiled up the mountain, with a heavy load on his back. When he reached them, he lowered his burden to the ground, and drank in the fresh mountain air in great breaths. Dr. Classen gave the man a coin, and, tipping his hat, the fellow went away.

All this while Heidi sat staring at the great bundle, too polite to ask what was in it, but dying to know.

"This is the something that was my companion from Frankfurt," said the doctor, drawing Heidi towards the big bale, from which he loosened the heavy outside wrappings. "There, now. Go to work, child, and discover the hidden treasures for yourself."

Heidi needed no second invitation, and when everything was spread about, stood staring at her gifts as if she could not believe her eyes. The doctor removed the cover from the box and showed her the cakes for the blind grandmother to eat with her coffee.

Now Heidi found words. "Cakes! for the grandmother!" she shouted, jumping about joyously. All the other things were quickly piled together to put away, but she would take the cake box at once down the Alm. Her grandfather persuaded her, however, to wait until evening, when they would both go down with their guest to Dorfli. Then Heidi found the bag of tobacco for the grandfather, which she quickly brought to him. Of course it had to be sampled at once, and the two men sat with their pipes, puffing out great clouds of smoke.

After examining her treasures again and again, Heidi came to stand before the men, and when there was a pause in their conversation, she said decidedly, "There is nothing that has given me more pleasure than the arrival of the doctor."

The two laughed at this announcement, but the old doctor was deeply touched. At sunset the guest started down to secure his lodging in Dorfli. Heidi skipped at his side while the Alm-Uncle followed with the box of cakes, the shawl, and the big sausage. When they reached goat-Peter's cottage, they left Heidi, and went on towards Dorfli, but she called after the doctor hastily, "Tomorrow will you go with the goats to the pasture?" for that was the loveliest place in the world to her.

"Indeed, I would like to, Heidi, if you will go with me," he answered, and so it was settled.

It took Heidi three trips to carry the gifts which her grandfather had left on the doorstep in the cottage: the box of cakes, the warm woollen shawl and the huge sausage. She carried them right to the grandmother, so that the old woman could feel them at once. The shawl she placed on her knees.

"They all come from Frankfurt, sent by Klara and Grandmamma," she explained to the wondering women. Brigitte was there also, but so taken by surprise that she never thought of helping the child, but let her carry in all the heavy things unaided.

"Don't the cakes make you very glad, Grandmother? Feel how soft they are!" Heidi cried over and over.

"What good people, Heidi! How kind they are!" the old woman replied, and she kept feeling the soft shawl, saying, "Who would have ever believed I should have anything so splendid for the cold winter!"

Heidi did not understand why the shawl gave more pleasure to the grandmother than the cakes. The sausage lay on the kitchen table, and Peter's mother regarded it with awe. She had never seen such a giant sausage in her life, and it really belonged to them, and they were going to eat it! She could not get over it.

Peter now came running in. "The Alm-Uncle is behind me. Heidi is to —" His eyes fell on the sausage, and he stood there transfixed.

But Heidi knew what he'd meant to say, so she extended her hand to the grandmother. The Alm-Uncle never went by the cottage now without coming in to say a word of cheer to his friends. But today it was late, and Heidi, as usual, had been up with the sun. So her grandfather only said, "The child must go to her sleep." Then he called a goodnight through the open door, took the waiting Heidi by the hand, and together they climbed the mountain under the starry heavens to their peaceful hut, high up on the Alm.

Chapter 17

THE HEALING ALM

EARLY next morning Peter came up with his goats as usual,
and with him came the doctor. This good man had done
his best to talk to the goatherd but Peter was no talker, and
finally even the doctor had to give up trying to make conversation with him. So it was silent company that clambered
up the steep hillside to the Alm-hut, where Heidi waited
for them in the golden sunshine with her goats.

"Are you coming with us?" Peter asked, repeating his
daily question.

"Yes, I am, if the doctor will go along," Heidi answered.
Peter eyed the doctor a little dubiously.

The Alm-Uncle now came from the hut to greet his guest
warmly. Then he hung the lunch bag over Peter's shoulder.
It was heavier than usual, for there was a large piece of the
delicious dried meat in it. Peter grinned with satisfaction,
as the weight of the bag promised some unusual luxury.

Bidding the Alm-Uncle goodbye, they began the ascent,
the goats at once surrounding Heidi, each one wishing for
the place beside her. Laughing, Heidi worked her way out
of the flock to run back to the doctor, and take his hand in
hers. With her there was no lack of conversation, for she
began at once on the droll little goats, skipped to the flowers
and the rocks, the birds and the snow field, so that the time
flew, and they reached the summit without knowing it.
Meanwhile Peter had cast many a jealous glance sidewise
at the doctor. He did not like to share Heidi's attention
with anyone, least of all with a stranger.

When they reached their usual resting place, Heidi took
the doctor to where the view was finest and pulled him
down on the grass. The heights above and the green valley

below glimmered in the golden autumn sunshine. From some pasture below the faint tinkling of cow bells floated sweetly and softly like a song of peace, and all the air was filled with happy sounds. The great snow field gleamed above, while grey old Falkniss raised rocky towers majestically against the blue, blue sky. Overhead the great eagle flew in wide graceful circles, not screaming today but gliding silently through the air.

Heidi looked at the doctor, her eyes sparkling from all the beauty, and hoping her old friend saw it all as she did.

The doctor looked down at the child. "Yes, dear, it is all lovely here, but how can one with a sad heart rejoice?"

"Oh," Heidi exclaimed, "no one here has a sad heart! They only have sad hearts in Frankfurt."

The doctor smiled fleetingly. Then he said, "Suppose someone came here from Frankfurt bringing his sad heart with him. What could be done to help him, Heidi?"

"Such a person should tell all his troubles to the good God," she replied promptly.

"That is a fine thought, my child. But if his sorrow comes from God, what then can he say to the Lord?"

Heidi considered this a while, seeking an answer from her own experience.

"One must wait," she said then, "and one must think that soon the good God will bring something to make one happier. All at once it will be quite plain how God has something good in his thoughts all the time, though we do not know it."

"That is a beautiful belief, Heidi," the doctor said. "Keep it always." He sat silent, gazing up at the rocky peaks and down into the shining vally. Then he added, as if to himself, "And yet it is possible to have a great shadow over one's eyes and not see all this beauty. Can you understand that, little Heidi?"

A sharp pain shot through Heidi's heart at these words. The great shadow of which the doctor spoke brought the blind grandmother to her mind. The poor old woman could never again see the bright sun, nor all the beauty of the world about her. It was a grief to the child, whenever she thought of it. So now she said earnestly, "Yes, I can understand that, but I know something which can lift the shadow. The grandmother's hymns. They make everything bright and cheerful again."

"Why hymns, Heidi? Say them for me. I, too, should like to hear them," the doctor said gravely.

Folding her hands in her lap, the little girl thought for a little, and then she began, her voice sweet and clear and pure as the mountain air she breathed.

Verse after verse she recited, until suddenly she was no longer sure that the doctor was listening. He had covered his face with his hands and sat so motionless that the child thought he had fallen asleep.

But he was not asleep. Heidi's words had carried him back to the distant past. He was a boy again, at his dear mother's knee, and she was repeating the same lines Heidi had just been saying – a hymn he had not heard for many years. So he sat motionless, lost in thought. When at last he recollected himself, he saw the child's wondering gaze, and taking her little hand he said, with a more cheerful ring in his voice, "Heidi, your hymn is beautiful. We will come here again, and you shall repeat it for me."

During all this time, goat-Peter had seethed with anger. It was so long since Heidi had been to the pasture with him, and now here she was sitting with that old doctor, and with never a word for him. It was more than Peter could endure; it vexed him and he made the most frightful faces, which, fortunately, neither the doctor nor Heidi saw.

Noting by the sun that it was now time for their midday meal, Peter shouted unceremoniously, and as loudly as he could, "It's time to eat! It's time to eat!"

Heidi jumped up at once, to bring the bag to the doctor, but he declared he was not hungry, and would drink only a little milk, and then climb farther up the mountain. Heidi immediately decided that she was not hungry, either, and would only drink some milk. Furthermore, she would guide the doctor to the great moss-grown stone where Thistlebird once had almost fallen over. She ran to Peter to explain this decision and to ask that he get them some milk from Schwänli.

The goatherd stared at Heidi in amazement, and then blurted, "Who will have what is in the lunch bag, then?"

"You may," she said, "but first bring the milk."

Never had Peter accomplished any task faster than this. As soon as the others had begun to drink their milk, he opened the lunch bag and snatched out the food, trembling with joy.

Having finished their milk, Heidi and the doctor went wandering over the pasture, and the golden autumn hours slipped away pleasantly.

At last the doctor had to take leave of his little companion, sending her back to goat-Peter and his flock while he himself went down the mountain. But as he turned to look back, he saw the child, still standing where he had left her, waving her hand, just as his own little daughter had done every day when he left the house.

The whole month was filled with beautiful, clear days, and each morning the doctor climbed up the Alm. Frequently he went on long rambles with the Uncle, high up among the rocks, where the eagles nested. The doctor marvelled at the knowledge of the old mountain man, and found the greatest pleasure in his conversation. He knew all the mountain herbs and their healing powers, and where they grew. He knew the habits of the animals there, and told many amusing stories of the tricks they played. The time passed so quickly, that evening surprised both men on every occasion they spent together, and each time the doctor left regretfully.

But on the finest days, the doctor chose to go with Heidi to the pasture. They sat together companionably on the Alm, and the child repeated her hymns and songs, and shared with her old friend all her bits of knowledge, and all her thoughts. Peter sat behind them, but he no longer resented the good doctor from Frankfurt.

So the doctor's holiday month drew to an end. One morning he came up with his face clouded. He must return to his duties in Frankfurt, he said, but he hated to leave, for he now loved the Alm and his friends there. The Alm-Uncle was sorry, too, for he had become much attached to the good doctor; and as for Heidi, she did not know what she would do without her dear old friend.

"Come down a little way with me, Heidi," begged the doctor, when he had said adieu to the Uncle, and Heidi put her hand in his, and off they went.

But at last the real parting came. "Now you must go back to your grandfather, child," and the doctor patted Heidi's black curls tenderly, "and I must go, too. Oh, Heidi! how I wish I could take you with me, and keep you always!"

At this, Heidi remembered Frankfurt – and too clearly the many houses, the endless stone streets, Miss Rotten-meier and Tinette. She said, rather doubtfully, "I'd like it better if you stayed with us."

"Yes, that would be better," he admitted, "but, alas, it cannot be, so farewell, Heidi," and the doctor held out his hand to her. Looking up into his face Heidi saw that his eyes were filled with tears, and he turned away quickly to go down the mountain.

Heidi stood still. His loving eyes, and the tears touched her tender heart. Suddenly she burst into loud weeping, and ran after her friend, calling, "Doctor, Doctor!"

He turned, just as Heidi flung herself into his arms, tears streaming down her woebegone face as she sobbed out, "I will go with you to Frankfurt, and I'll stay as long as you want me, but first let me tell my grandfather."

"Dear, dear child," the doctor soothed her gently. "No, Heidi," he said tenderly, "not just now. You must stay under the pines a while longer or you will soon be ill again. But if I am ever sick and alone, will you come to me then, and stay with me, so that I shall have someone to love and care for me?"

"Yes, yes! I will surely come, for I love you almost as much as I do my grandfather," she said, still sobbing.

After hugging her fondly, the doctor turned away, while Heidi stood and waved farewell as long as she could see him.

He was almost happy now, and as he turned to look at Heidi for the last time, before she was hidden from view by a turn in the road, he murmured, "It is good for body and soul up there, on the mountain, and makes life seem worth living."

Chapter 18

WINTER IN DORFLI

A FEW weeks later, the snow lay piled up about the Alm-hut, so that it seemed as if the windows touched the ground. Below them nothing of the building could be seen and the house door had quite disappeared. If the Alm-Uncle had been up there, he would have had to do as Peter did at his cottage, for it now snowed hard almost every night.

Every morning, Peter jumped out of the bedroom window into the snow, then fought his way through the drifts. His mother tossed the broom down to him from the window and he brushed and shoved the snow with it until he reached the house door, which he then had to clear thoroughly. If he ever failed to do so, it would fall in and half fill the kitchen when any one tried to enter. And, if the snow were allowed to freeze hard, then no one could get in or out, because the house would be boxed-in solid. For Peter, however, this was not so bad, because if he had to go down to Dorfli, he crawled out of the window and lowered himself onto the snow crust. His mother then handed out his little sledge through the same window, and seating himself on it he could whizz away, for all paths led down to the village.

But the Uncle was not on the Alm this winter, for he had kept his promise. As soon as the first snow fell, he closed the hut and the shed, and taking Heidi and the goats he went down to Dörfli.

Near the church there stood an old, dilapidated building, which once had been a spacious mansion. Some of the rooms were still in fair condition, though other parts of the house had fallen into decay. No one had lived in this house for many years, for unless one knew how to prop up the falling walls, repair the windows, and mend the holes and gaps as they appeared, it was not really habitable, since the Dörfli winters were so long and cold. But the Alm-Uncle knew exactly how to make himself comfortable. He rented the old house, as soon as he had decided to go down to the village, and through the autumn he went there frequently to put it in order, and make it snug for the winter. In mid-October he moved down there with his little family.

In one part of the tumble-down house, just off the old courtyard, the Uncle had made a partition of boards, and covered the floor with straw, as a lodging for his goats. In another he had found a room with a strong oaken door still hanging firmly on its hinges. It was a fine large room, in good condition with its dark oak panelling unbroken. A huge stove stood in a corner, reaching almost to the ceiling, and covered with white tiles on which blue pictures were painted – old castles and towers, surrounded by tall trees, hunters and their dogs, and even a quiet lake under wide shadowing oaks, where a fisherman sat with his rod over the water. A bench circled the whole stove, so that one could sit at ease to study the pictures. This pleased Heidi enormously.

As soon as her grandfather showed her this room, she ran to the stove, and began to admire the pictures. As she slid along the bench, she at last came behind the stove, when something new caught her interest. Between the stove and the wall was a wide space, and there some boards formed a rack that might have been used for drying apples. Here, instead of apples, Heidi found her bed, made up exactly as it had been on the Alm – a high pile of hay, with the sheet well tucked in all around, and the sack for a coverlet. "Oh, Grandfather," Heidi shouted, "this must be my bedroom! How wonderful! But where's yours? Where will you sleep?"

"Your bed must be near the stove, where you won't freeze. Come and see mine, now."

Heidi skipped through the long room behind her grandfather, until he opened a door at the other end, to a smaller room where his bed was placed. Still another door led from this room, and opening it curiously, Heidi stood in surprise.

Before her extended a huge kitchen. Although the grandfather had worked mightily to make this room usable, there still remained much to be done. There were still holes and cracks on every side, but many had already been filled with boards and planks, and the big old door had been made fast with nails and wires, so that now it could be shut securely.

Heidi felt pleased with their new dwelling, and by the time Peter came to see her the next day, she had peeped into every corner and was so perfectly at home, that she could show him all about the place.

The child slept soundly in her warm nook behind the stove, but every morning, when she awakened, she thought herself on the Alm, and when she realized that she was not, she had a choking and stifled feeling, until presently she heard her grandfather talking to the goats, and heard them bleating, as if saying, "Come out, Heidi! Hurry, now! We're waiting." Then she knew where she was, and sprang up and dressed as quickly as possible, and ran out to the stalls. On the fourth day in Dorfli, however, she announced that she must go to see the grandmother, who ought not to be neglected so long.

But the grandfather shook his head to this. "The Alm is

deep in snow, and it is still snowing there. If Peter can scarcely fight his way through it, a little one like my Heidi, would be snowed under in no time. Wait until it freezes. Then you can walk up on the crust."

It troubled Heidi that she could not go up on the Alm then and there, and yet the days were so filled with all sorts of things, that one was gone and another came almost without being noticed. Every morning and every afternoon she went to school, and learned her lessons eagerly. Peter, however, she seldom saw in the school, for he was rarely there.

The teacher, a rather mild man, only said now and then, "It seems to me that Peter is among the missing again today. But there is a good deal of snow up his way, and he probably can't get through."

Towards evening, when school was over, Peter came through easily enough, to pay his regular visit to Heidi.

After a few days, the sun shone again, and in the morning the whole Alm glistened like crystal.

When Peter opened his window and jumped into the snow as usual, it did not feel at all as he expected. Instead of sinking and floundering about, he came down hard on solid crust, and slipped and slid quite a distance before he could stop and right himself again. The whole Alm was frozen over, but Peter did not mind, for he knew that now Heidi could come up to the cottage, and he was content. Back in the cottage, he gulped down his milk, stuffed his bread into his pocket, and announced "Now I must go to school."

"Yes, go and study hard," his mother said.

Out of the window Peter crept this time, for the door was still blocked. Behind him, he drew his little sledge and down the mountain he shot like a rocket over the slippery crust. He flew along so fast that when he came to Dorfli, where the descent continued down to Mayenfeld, he went right on, for it would have required great effort to stop the speeding sledge in its course. So on he flew until he reached the plain, where the sledge stopped of its own accord.

He got off and looked about him. He had been carried even beyond Mayenfeld! Peter shrugged. School must have begun long ago, and it would be over before he could get up to Dörfli, as it would take him a full hour to climb the hill again. So he did not hurry to return, and when he did reach Dörfli, Heidi had just come home from school, and was sitting down to dinner with her grandfather. Peter went in, and promptly announced the thought uppermost in his mind. "We've got it," he said as soon as he swung the door open.

"What's that, General?" the Uncle, asked, quite puzzled.

"The crust," Peter replied.

"Oh! Now I can go up to see the grandmother," Heidi cried joyfully, for she had understood Peter's meaning at once. "But why didn't you come to school, Peter? You could have, on your sledge," she added reproachfully.

"Came down but went too far, and then it was too late," returned Peter.

"That is equal to deserting," the Uncle said severely, "and when men do that they should be taken by the ears, do you understand?"

Peter covered his ears in a great alarm. For he feared the Alm-Uncle when he used that tone.

"And you an officer," scolded the Uncle. "What would you do if your goats were to take it into their heads not to follow or obey you any more?"

"Beat them," said Peter.

"And if a boy behaved like an unruly goat, should he get beaten a little? What would you say to that?"

"Serve him right," was the answer.

"Well, now, you know what you deserve, Goat-general. The next time you go sliding down into the valley, instead of stopping at the school, you come back here, and I will give it to you."

Startled, Peter at last realized that the Uncle had compared him to an unruly goat, and he peered anxiously into the corners to see what there might be in them that the Alm-Uncle might plan to use on him!

However, the Uncle said quite pleasantly, "Sit down to table with us, and then Heidi will go up with you."

Peter obeyed at once, but now Heidi was so excited about seeing the grandmother that she could not eat. She pushed her potato and toasted cheese over to Peter who already had received a plateful from the Uncle, but he was quite equal to the extra helping and dug in at once.

Heidi ran to the cupboard to get the new warm cloak which Klara had sent her. Now she could make the journey, with the hood over her head, and be perfectly warm. She waited impatiently for Peter to finish, and as soon as he put the last bit in his mouth, she said, "Now, come Peter!" and off they went.

All the way up the mountain, Heidi chattered about Schwänli and Bärli, and how they would not eat in their new stalls on the first day. They hung their heads and made no sound, and when she asked her grandfather about it, he had told her that they felt as she did when she went to Frankfurt, for they had never come down from the Alm before in all their lives. "And Peter," Heidi added, "you ought to know just once, what that dreadful feeling is."

They had almost reached the cottage when Peter spoke for the first time – not about what Heidi had said, but on a thought entirely his own. "I'd rather go to school," he muttered, "than get from the Uncle what he promised to give me if I don't."

Heidi stared at him for a moment and then agreed heartily that from Peter's viewpoint, school would be much better.

They found Peter's mother sitting alone with her mending. The grandmother, she told Heidi, had to be in bed all day because it was too cold for her in the cottage. This was something new to Heidi, who had become used to finding her old friend seated in the corner at her spinning wheel.

She ran to the bedroom, where the old woman lay in her narrow bed, with its thin coverlet, and herself wrapped closely in the grey shawl.

"God be thanked!" cried the blind woman when she heard Heidi's bounding step on the floor. Ever since she had heard of the old gentleman from Frankfurt, who walked up to the Alm every day, she had feared that the child might be persuaded to return to the city with him, or some messenger might be sent for her. But here was her treasure again, come to visit.

Heidi stood by the bedside anxiously. "Are you ill, Grandmother?" she asked.

"No, child! But the cold has got into my old bones a bit, that's all," and she stroked the child's cheek fondly.

"Will you feel better then, when the weather is warm again?" Heidi asked.

"Yes, sooner than that, God willing. I must get to my spinning before long."

The worried Heidi relaxed somewhat, and then said. "In Frankfurt, Grandmother, they wear their shawls only to go walking, and never in bed."

"I know, Heidi, but I wear the shawl in bed to keep warm, for the bedclothes are rather thin."

Heidi considered that and noticed something else. "Your bed, Grandmother, it goes down at your head, instead of up."

"I know, child, and I feel it quite plainly myself." The old woman fumbled at her thin little pillow, trying to plump it up a little. "This never was a thick pillow, and now I have slept on it for so many years, it has become quite flattened out."

"Oh, if only I had asked Klara to give me my bed, to bring home with me!" Heidi wailed. "It had three enormous pillows. Could you sleep so high, Grandmother?"

"Yes, indeed, and I could breathe with my head high," replied the grandmother. "But we won't speak of that any more. I have so much to be thankful for: the fresh soft rolls every day, and this nice warm shawl, and your coming to see me, Heidi. Will you read to me today?"

"Of course, Grandmother!" and the little girl ran to get the book. She picked out one lovely hymn after another for she knew them all, and was happy to read them again and again.

The grandmother lay with folded hands, her face smoothed out and peaceful, as she listened.

At long last the child said, "It's getting dark, Grandmother, and I must go home. But I am so glad that you are feeling better."

Holding the child's hand tightly, the grandmother said, "Your visits always make me better, and when you read to me it makes my heart light and my spirit glad. God bless you, Heidi."

The grandmother let go the child's hand, and she ran out quickly. The night had already come, but outside the moon made it seem as bright as day. Peter settled himself on his sled, and with Heidi behind him, the two glided down the Alm as if they were birds flying.

Later, when Heidi lay on her soft bed of hay behind the warm stove, she thought again of the poor old blind grandmother, with her thin pillow and her hard bed, and the darkness that filled her spirit and made her heart heavy.

What could she do about that? Heidi thought and thought – and all at once it came to her! She knew what she could do, and now could hardly wait for the next day to put her new plan into practice.

She had been so busy thinking, that she had not yet said her prayers, which she never forgot. Now she prayed for her grandfather and for the blind grandmother, and then she turned on her side and slept soundly until morning.

Chapter 19

PETER MAKES A DISCOVERY

THE NEXT day Peter came down to school – on time – and brought his dinner in his satchel. When all the children who lived in Dorfli went home at noon, those who came from afar, as he did, ate their midday meal in the schoolroom. At one o'clock school began again, and for once, Peter got through an entire day in the schoolroom. When it was over, he went to visit Heidi at her grandfather's.

Heidi was waiting for him in the big room, and as he entered, she darted to him, saying, "You know what, Peter?"

"What?"

"You must learn to read," Heidi declared.

"Can't."

"Nonsense," Heidi said, sounding very grownup. "I don't believe that of you any longer. The grandmamma in Frankfurt knew that it wasn't true, and now I do, too."

Peter looked quite astonished at this news.

"I'll teach you to read. I know how to do it," continued Heidi, "and you must learn, and then read a hymn or two to the grandmother every day."

"No," grumbled Peter. "Won't."

His resistance against something that was good and right aroused Heidi's indignation. Her eyes flashing, she stood before the big boy, and said threateningly, "Then I will tell you what will happen to you! Your mother has already said that she wants you to go to Frankfurt to learn all sorts of things, and I know where the boys go to school there. Klara showed me the big schoolhouse when we were out driving one day. In Frankfurt they don't stop going to school when they grow up, but keep on even after they are great big men. I saw that myself. And there isn't even one kind teacher there, as we have here, either. Whole rows of masters go into the schoolhouse, and they're all dressed in black as if they were going to church. They wear tall black hats on their heads — so high," and Heidi motioned with her hands excitedly while cold shivers ran up and down her listener's back.

"Then you'll have to go in among all the masters," continued Heidi, really throwing herself into the recital, "and when your turn comes and you can't read, or even spell, then you'll see how the masters will laugh, and make fun of you. It'll be much worse than Tinette, and you just ought to know what it's like when she makes fun of you."

"Then I will learn," the boy said, half-scared, half-angry.

"That's better," Heidi's voice softened at once. "We'll begin right away," and she ran to get the necessary things together and drew Peter towards the table.

Among the many gifts that her dear Klara had sent from Frankfurt, there was one which had pleased Heidi very much. It was a little book of alphabet verses, and Heidi had thought of it when she was making plans to teach Peter. Now with their heads bent over the little book, the lesson began. Peter had to try to spell out the first verse again and again, for Heidi was determined to have it thoroughly learned. At last she said, "You can't do it yet, so I will read it over to you several times, and when you know what it means then you'll be able to spell it out more easily," and she read:

> Now learn your A B C right quick
> Or go and get walloped with a stick.

"I won't go," Peter said crossly.

"Where?" Heidi asked.

"To be walloped."

"Then learn your A B C right quick," Heidi advised.

So Peter really applied himself to the task, repeating the letters, until at last Heidi said, "Now you know A B C," and as she realized how much the verse had helped her pupil, she decided to prepare the way a little for the next lesson. So she read several more verses, slowly and clearly.

> For D, E, F and G, H, I
> You'd better train your tongue to try.
>
> Add J, K, L to what you know,
> Plus M and N, to dodge a blow.
>
> Remember P. Hold on to Q,
> Or it will go the worse for you.
>
> The letters next: R, S and T.
> The rest should follow easily.

Heidi stopped, for Peter was so quiet, she had to see what he was about. All these threats and mysterious warnings had frightened him so thoroughly that he did not dare stir, but sat staring at the little girl full of alarm. Her tender heart was touched, and she said, "Don't be frightened, Peter. If you will come to me every afternoon I will teach you. And if you learn as fast as you did today, you will soon know all the letters, and you won't need to worry about a thing in the verses."

Peter promised meekly. Every afternoon thereafter, he followed his little teacher's orders faithfully, and soon he did know most of his letters by heart, and the verses too.

The grandfather often sat in the room with the pair, smoking his pipe and listening, the corners of his mouth twitching frequently because goat-Peter was so droll. The lad was generally rewarded with an invitation to supper, and this always cheered him after his tremendous exertions.

The winter days passed and at last they reached the letter V, and Heidi read:

> Mistake a U for V just once
> And you'll be written down a dunce.

"See if I do!" Peter growled. But for all the defiant talk

he studied hard, as if he expected someone might come up from behind to take him by the collar and write him off as a dunce.

Next evening came:

> Imprint the W on your wits
> Or you're the next the master hits!

"There isn't any stick," the lad said triumphantly.

"Then you don't know what my grandfather has in his chest. If that great stick, as thick as my arm, should be taken out, I think we'd stay clear of the master."

Now that Peter thought of it, he did know that hazel stick! and he bent over his W until he learned it.

> Just keep your thoughts on X, I say,
> If you would like to eat today.

Peter looked quickly towards the cupboard where the bread and cheese were kept, and muttered, "I never said I was going to forget my X, did I?"

"Well, if you won't, we can learn another letter today, and that's the last but one," and Heidi read:

> And if the Y's a stumbling block,
> You'll find yourself a laughing-stock!

Instantly, before Peter's eyes, rose all the blackrobed masters of Frankfurt, with their tall hats on their heads, and scorn on their faces. He learned Y so thoroughly that he knew it even with his eyes shut.

The next day, with the last letter before him, Peter was in rather a high and mighty mood, so when patient Heidi read:

> If Z ties you up in knots
> They'll send you to the Hottentots!

he said scornfully, "Hah! nobody knows where to find the Hottentots."

"Is that so? My grandfather knows. He's visiting the

pastor so I'll run over and ask him." And Heidi jumped up to run to the door.

"Wait!" screamed Peter, feeling as if already the Alm-Uncle and the pastor were coming to send him to the Hottentots.

"What is the matter with you?" Heidi asked, astonished.

"Nothing! Come back! I will learn it," Peter babbled.

Heidi shrugged. She had begun to be curious about what a Hottentot was, and was going over to find out. But Peter sounded so desperate that she came back to him, exacting extra work for her return. Not only did he master Z, but Heidi forced him into words of one syllable, and Peter learned more that evening than he had ever done before.

The snow had softened again, and more fell every day, so that three weeks went by and Heidi did not get up to see the grandmother. She worked all the harder with Peter, so that he might be able to read the hymns to the old lady.

One evening the boy came home and announced in his usual fashion, "I know how now."

"What do you know, Peterkin?" his mother asked.

"How to read."

"Peterkin! Is it possible? Mother, did you hear?" cried Brigitte.

The grandmother heard and marvelled. How had this come about?

"I must read you a hymn. Heidi said I must," Peter told his grandmother.

Brigitte ran to bring the book, and Peter began to read aloud. As he paused after each verse, his mother said, "Who would have believed it!"

The blind grandmother listened intently, but she said nothing.

The very next day, Peter's class at school had a reading lesson. When his turn came, the teacher sighed a little and asked, "Shall we skip you, Peter, as usual, or will you try out a line or two?"

Peter stood up and read three whole lines without a single mistake.

The teacher set down his book to stare dumbfounded at the boy as if he had never heard reading before. "Peter," he said at last, "how did this miracle happen?"

"Heidi," answered the lad.

Even more amazed, the teacher looked at Heidi.

"I have noticed a change in your attendance, also," continued the master. "You've been coming to school every day. Who has worked that change in you?"

"Uncle," Peter replied with his usual briefness.

With increasing astonishment the teacher looked from Peter to Heidi, and back again. Then he said cautiously, as if creeping up on the idea, "You may read again."

Peter did so, correctly and without any fuss. He had indeed learned to read.

As soon as he had dismissed school, the master hurried to the pastor to tell him what had happened that day, and to point out what a good influence Heidi and her grandfather were.

Every evening, at home, Peter now read aloud one hymn. In that he obeyed Heidi, but he never offered to read a second, nor did his grandmother ever ask him to repeat anything.

Brigitte's delight, however, knew no bounds, and after Peterkin was asleep, she would say proudly, "Now that Peterkin has learned to read, there's no knowing what wonderful things he may do next."

"Yes," said her mother one night, with a little sigh, "it is well for Peter that he has learned something, but I hope spring will not be long in coming so that I may have Heidi again. Something is left out so often when Peterkin reads to me. I think about it, and then I lose the place, and the words don't do me the good that they do when Heidi reads them."

The truth of the matter was that Peter, in order to make the reading easier for himself, left out all the long words!

"There are enough left," he thought, "and the grandmother will never miss them." So, naturally, the meaning of the hymns was changed considerably by Peter's way of reading them.

Chapter 20

THE GUESTS FROM FRANKFURT

At last it was the month of May. Mountain brooks, fed by the melting snows, rushed and leaped down into the valley. In the warm sunshine, the Alm grew greener day by day. Fresh new grass and the early spring flowers opened hourly to the sun's quickening rays. Spring breezes rustled through the old pines, shaking out last year's rusty needles, to make room for the bright green new ones, and high above, the great eagle spread wide his wings against the blue sky.

Heidi was on the Alm again. She ran everywhere, eager to see everything, to hear the wind in the pines, and to shout along with it as it rustled through the tossing branches. Then away to the other side of the hut, and the sun-bathed grass, to search for the timid flowerbuds and count those already opened, and to breathe deeply of the scented air, as it rose from the fresh, moist earth. The Alm had never been so beautiful as now, she thought.

From the workshop in the bed behind the hut, there came the busy sounds of hammer and of saw – dear, homey and familiar. Of course she had to know on what her grandfather was working so busily, so into the shop she ran on nimble feet. Just outside the door she found a new chair, spick and span, and another one, almost finished, in her grandfather's skilful hands.

"I know what these are for!" cried Heidi joyfully. "They will be needed when everybody comes from Frankfurt.

This one is for Grandmamma, and that one for dear Klara. Do you suppose there will have to be another," she went on falteringly, "or do you think that Miss Rottenmeier will not come?"

"I cannot tell, child, but it will be safer to have one ready, so that we can invite her to take a seat, if she should come."

While Heidi stood looking at the chairs, she heard the daily shrill whistle and shout. She ran out of the workshop and was at once surrounded by the bleating flock. Each of the goats showed plainly that it, too, was glad to be back on the Alm again.

Peter ploughed through them all, for he had something to give to Heidi.

"There!" he said, thrusting a letter towards her, without any further explanation.

"Did you find this up in the pasture, Peter!" she asked, astonished.

"No."

"Where then?"

"In the lunch bag."

Which was quite true. The night before, the postman in Dorfli had given the letter to Peter, to take up to the Alm. Peter had put it in his empty satchel. The next morning, his bread and cheese went on top of it, and went up the Alm with his goats, as usual. Of course he had seen the Uncle and Heidi on his way up, but it wasn't until he had eaten his dinner, and saw the letter in the bottom of his satchel that he thought of it again.

Heidi read the address carefully, and then ran back to her grandfather in the shop.

"A letter from Frankfurt, from Klara!" she cried in high glee. "Will you listen while I read it, Grandfather?"

The Uncle nodded that he was ready to hear it, and so was Peter, who leaned his back against the doorpost, uninvited, but thus prepared for the strain of listening.

"Dear Heidi:

Everything is packed for the journey, and in two or three more days we hope to start. Papa cannot come with us, for he must go directly to Paris.

Dr. Classen comes every day, and even before he enters my room, he calls out, 'Away! away! You must go! Off to the Alm!' He is impatient to get us off. I wish you could know how much he enjoyed his visit with you on the Alm. All through the winter he has been here almost every day, and every day he has told me about it. About the mountains and the flowers, and the fresh, pure air. 'Anybody would get well there!' he has said again and again. He is different, too, since his visit to you – bouncy and cheerful.

How glad I am, too, at the thought of seeing all the things he has told about, and of being with you on the Alm, and of meeting Peter and his goats! But first I have to take some treatments for six weeks in Ragatzbad, as the doctor has ordered. And then we shall find lodgings in Dorfli, so that in fine weather I can be carried up the Alm to stay all day with you. Grandmamma will be with me. She is eager to see you again.

But Miss Rottenmeier will not come. Grandmamma used to invite her almost every day, saying, 'Do not hesitate to say so, if you wish to go with us Rottenmeier.' But she always thanked my grandmamma in a terribly polite fashion, and said that she did not wish to impose upon her kindness. I knew what she was thinking of! Sebastian gave a frightful account of the Alm, when he came back from taking you home. He said terrible rocks hung over the path, the road went up so steeply, he said, that there was danger of tumbling over backwards. Goats, perhaps, but certainly not people, could ever climb up there without risking life and limb.

Miss Rottenmeier shuddered all through his recital and did not seem to care at all for a Swiss journey thereafter. Tinette, too, has been frightened, and won't go with me. So we shall come quite alone, Grandmamma and I, although

Sebastian will be with us as far as Ragatz, and then return to Frankfurt.

I can hardly wait until I see you.

Farewell, dearest Heidi. Grandmamma sends you a thousand good wishes with her love.

Your true friend,
Klara"

As soon as Heidi finished reading, Peter darted away, swinging his rod and making it whistle angrily in the air. Down the mountain scampered the startled goats, while the lad still slashed at his invisible enemy. This enemy, of course, was the expected company from Frankfurt, and the goatherd was already very bitter about it.

Heidi, on the other hand, was so full of joyous anticipation, that she planned a visit to the grandmother for the very next day to tell her about the letter, and the visitors from Frankfurt.

The grandmother was no longer in bed, but sitting again in her corner at her spinning. She had a strange expression on her face, as if her thoughts were troubled.

She had not slept well the previous night, haunted by the same anxiety, aroused when Peter had come home full of anger. What he had been angry about was not very clear to the old woman, but she had gathered that a crowd of people were coming from Frankfurt to the Alm. What would happen then, the grandmother wondered uneasily. All sorts of unpleasant possibilities rose in her mind.

Now Heidi came bounding in, full of energy and chatter about the visitors. But all of a sudden she interrupted herself, saying, "What is the matter, Grandmother? Aren't you pleased for me?"

"Yes, yes, Heidi, I am pleased for your sake," replied the grandmother, trying to look more cheerful.

"But you are worried about something," Heidi insisted.

"No, no, it is nothing," the old woman said soothingly. "Give me your hand, Heidi, so that I can feel that you are

159

really here. It would surely be for your good," she added, "though how I could live through it again I don't see."

Heidi did not know what the grandmother meant, but she said anyway, "I will have nothing for my good that you can't live through, Grandmother," and said it so decidedly that a new worry arose in the grandmother's mind.

The old woman now was sure that the people from Frankfurt were coming to take Heidi back with them, since the child was well and strong again. She knew that it would be good for her to go. This was the very cause of the grandmother's anxiety. But she realized that she must not let Heidi know of it, lest the affectionate child, for her sake, should refuse to go. So, casting about for something that would lift up her heart, she said, "Dear, Heidi, read me the hymn which begins with 'God will provide'."

Heidi at once brought down the old hymnbook, and read from it in her sweet, clear voice, until the old lady began to look much happier.

"Yes, that is exactly what I needed," said the grandmother, "God will provide everything just as it should be; only we must trust Him. Read it again, Heidi, so that I will not forget it," and the child read the lines once more, and again to the blind grandmother.

In the evening, as Heidi climbed up the Alm towards home, with the bright stars coming out, one by one, she repeated aloud the words she had just read: "God will provide", and a warm glow filled her own heart.

The green month of May passed into balmy June, with its long, sun-filled days, when all the flowers on the Alm burst into fragrant bloom.

One day, towards the end of June, after her household tasks were finished, Heidi ran out of the hut to see if the great bush of star-thistles was in bloom. But first she looked down into the valley and as she did so, she gave a sudden shout which brought the Uncle out of his shop.

"Grandfather! Grandfather!" cried the child, quite beside herself. "Come here! Look! Look down the mountain!"

The grandfather did so, and his eyes widened, for an extraordinary sight was there below – a procession wending its slow way up the quiet Alm.

First came two men, carrying a sedan chair, in which a young girl sat enveloped in many wraps and shawls. Then came a horse with a stately lady on his back, who looked about her in a lively fashion. The wheel chair, so well known to Heidi, came next, and then a porter with a basket piled high with rugs, furs and shawls.

"They're here! they're here!" screamed Heidi, jumping up and down; and there they were indeed, coming nearer and nearer every moment, until at last they reached the grass in front of the hut. The bearers set the sedan chair on the ground, and Heidi rushed to kiss and hug her Klara.

The grandmamma came up on her horse and descended, and Heidi ran to greet her tenderly. Then the lady turned to the Alm-Uncle, who bade her welcome, and instantly the two seemed like old friends.

"My dear Uncle," exclaimed Grandmamma, "what a glorious place you have here! A king might well envy you. And Heidi – how blooming and how lovely, like a rose!" She drew the child to her and stroked her sun-browned cheek. "What do you say to all this, Klara?"

"It's so beautiful, so beautiful," Klara said, looking about her with the greatest pleasure. "Oh, Grandmamma, if I could only stay here always!"

Meanwhile, the Alm-Uncle had rolled the wheel chair close and spread the shawls and soft rugs over it. "It would be better for the child to be in her own chair than in the litter," he said, and lifting her gently from the sedan, he placed her comfortably, covering her up with rugs and tucking them in about her feet, as if nursing were his business.

The grandmamma looked on, amazed. "My dear Uncle," she cried, "that was well done. I wish all nurses were as skilful in handling invalids."

The Uncle smiled a little, for he had felt at once that Klara was his special charge.

The sky was deep blue and cloudless over the hut, and far away above the pine trees, the high cliffs rose in shimmering grey against it. Klara could not look about her enough.

"Oh, Heidi, if I could only run about as you do!" she cried longingly. "If I could go with you to look at everything that I have heard so much about, and never seen!"

Instantly Heidi was behind the chair and, giving it a mighty push, rolled it over the short, smooth grass, under the pines. Klara had never seen such giant trees as these. The grandmamma, too, was filled with admiration.

Heidi next rolled the chair to the goat stalls, but here there was not much to be seen, for the animals were away. Disappointed, Klara said, "Oh, Grandmamma, I want to see Schwänli and Bärli, and all the other goats, and Peter! I won't be able to if we have to go down as early as you said we must."

"Enjoy whatever you can, dear child, and don't bewail what may escape you," the grandmamma said, following the chair that Heidi was pushing quite easily now.

"The flowers!" Klara exclaimed. "Whole bushes of them! and all the noddng bluebells. If I could just get out and pick them!"

Heidi darted to the flowers, and brought back a huge bouquet. "These are nothing," she said, handing them to Klara. "If you go up with us to the pasture, there you will see something! It's covered with them. Red star-thistle, sand bluebells, and thousands of bright yellow flowers, that make the field look as if it were pure gold. My grandfather says that those are called sun's eyes. Everything smells so good! If you once sit down you never want to get up and leave, it is so lovely there!"

Klara's gentle blue eyes seemed to catch fire from Heidi's. "Could I get up there?" she asked. "Could I get up so high? If I could only walk, Heidi, and climb the Alm with you. I've never wanted to so much before."

"I'll push you in your chair, everywhere I can," Heidi promised, trying to comfort Klara.

While the girls and the grandmamma stood under the pines, the Alm-Uncle had brought out table and chairs for dinner, and set about cooking the meal. Soon he had everything served, and the company seated.

The grandmamma was quite enchanted with their dining room. "I've never enjoyed anything as much as this," she declared. "It's truly glorious." She glanced at Klara and exclaimed, "What's this! Klara are you really eating a second piece of cheese?"

Klara nodded, her mouth full. When she had swallowed more the of the golden toasted cheese, she said, "It all tastes better than everything put together in Ragatz, the cheese, the bread – everything!"

"That is the effect of our mountain air," the Alm-Uncle said, smiling and well pleased.

Sometime after dinner, the grandmamma glanced towards the west, and said, "We must soon get ready to go down again, Klara. The sun is setting, and the people will be here with my horse and your sedan chair."

At this Klara's happy face clouded. "Oh, Grandmamma, we have not been in the hut yet, or seen Heidi's bed. Oh, if the day were only ten hours longer!"

The grandmamma smiled sympathetically. She wished to see the hut herself, she said. The little company rose from the table at once, and the Alm-Uncle rolled the chair towards the door. It was far too wide to pass through, so he lifted Klara out and carried her into the hut in his strong arms.

Inside, the grandmamma looked everywhere with the most lively interest. The housekeeping, she said, was indeed very neat and well-ordered.

"Heidi's bed must be up there!" she added, and nimbly climbed the little ladder to the hayloft. "How sweet it smells here! Oh, it must be a very healthful bedroom!" she exclaimed and went to the opening to look outside, while the Uncle came up with Klara on his arm, and Heidi right along behind.

Klara was enchanted by the charm of Heidi's bedroom. "How perfect it is for you here, Heidi!" she exclaimed. "From your bed you can look straight into the sky, and the hay smells so sweet all about, and the sound of the wind in the pines – I could never grow tired of listening to it."

The Uncle turned to the grandmamma. "If you would entrust Klara to our care for a time – allow her to stay here – I believe she would gain new strength. The many shawls and rugs which came up with her could be used to make a comfortable bed, right here, next to Heidi's. It really would be quite simple."

The two girls held their breath and suddenly screamed with delight at such an arrangement. The grandmamma's eyes twinkled as she nodded.

"My dear Uncle," she said, "How did you know what I was thinking of, and hoping you'd suggest? Only the knowledge of the nursing and the tending stopped me from asking you! I thank you, with all my heart," she added, taking his hand warmly in hers.

The Uncle beamed at her and at the shouting girls, then set to work at once. First he carried Klara back to her chair before the hut and left her with Heidi. Then he gathered up all the shawls and rugs and climbed back to the loft.

While the grandmamma watched, he spread these, one on top of the other, over the fragrant hay.

She reached down and passed her hand over the bed. It was soft and springy and inviting. "Klara will certainly be comfortable here," the lady declared, quite satisfied, and climbed down to rejoin the children.

The girls were already deep in plans of what they would do from morning to night all the time they were to be together. How long would that be? they clamoured to know.

The grandmamma turned to the Uncle and he replied that four weeks would allow them to judge if the air on the Alm helped to strengthen Klara, or not.

Now the girls hugged each other wildly, for they had never expected to be together that long.

At this moment the sedan-chair bearers and the horse came toiling up the mountain path. The sedan chair went back empty; the grandmamma was escorted down by the Uncle, holding the bridle rein, for the descent was steep and not without danger.

"I'll come back and visit you now and then," the grandmamma told the girls before she left, "to see what you are about. I know the time won't lie heavy on your hands."

"No! Not for a minute!" they shouted and waved and waved as she departed.

The grandmamma had decided to return to Ragatzbad, and from there undertake her Alpine visits from time to time. There was no need for her to stay in Dorfli. She knew her Klara could not be in better hands, or in a better climate.

Peter came down from the pasture with his goats before the Uncle came up again. As soon as the animals spied Heidi, they ran towards her as usual, and in a moment, Klara, in her chair, was also surrounded by the curious, bleating creatures. Heidi named and presented them to her friend as fast as she could, and Klara soon learned who pretty Snowball was, and Thistlebird, the grandfather's well-kept stock, and even the big bold Turk.

Peter, meanwhile, stood to one side and glared at the happy newcomer.

When the children at last looked towards him and called out, "Good evening, Peter," he made no answer. Instead, he slashed at the air with his rod as if he would like to cut it all to bits, and then ran off, the little army of goats at his heels.

"That Peter," said Heidi, shaking her dark curls, "sometimes even I don't understand him. Tomorrow he will be in a better humour."

Of all the wonders of the Alm, the best for Klara came at the end of the day, when she lay in the big soft bed, up in the hayloft, next to Heidi, and looked through the round opening into the starry heavens.

"Oh, Heidi," she breathed, "it's like driving in a high open carriage, right through the sky. I wouldn't have missed this for anything – not anything in the whole, whole world."

For a long while they lay silently and watched the stars, and then, Heidi said, "We must not go to sleep forgetting our prayers."

So they sat up and prayed to the good God and thanked Him for allowing them to be together, and for all the other good things He had brought into their lives. And then Heidi put one arm under her head, and in the next moment fell fast asleep.

Klara, however, lay awake for a long, long time in this wonderful bedroom under the stars. In all her life she had scarcely seen the stars at all, for she never went out of the house at night, and the heavy house curtains were always drawn long before the stars shone above Frankfurt. So now Klara could not look enough at the shimmering heavens – until her eyes closed of their own accord.

times even I don't understand him. Tomorrow he will be in a better humour."

Of all the wonders of the Alm, the one best for Klara came

Chapter 21

PLEASANT DAYS ON THE ALM

THE SUN was just climbing over the tops of the mountains when the Alm-Uncle came out of the hut, as he did every morning, to see the silvery mist melt away, and the world emerge from the shadows as the new day awoke.

When the sun came out in its full glory and poured its golden light over the rocks and woods and hilltops, the Uncle went back into the hut and mounted the little ladder to the hayloft. Klara had opened her eyes, and was watching the sunbeams dance on her bed, but Heidi was still asleep.

The grandfather smiled at her. "Have you slept well? Do you feel rested?" he asked.

"Oh, yes," Klara assured him. Once asleep, she had not awakened through the night.

This pleased the grandfather and he began at once to help Klara get dressed, as handily as if he had cared for sick children all his life.

By the time Heidi awakened, her grandfather was ready to carry Klara down the ladder. Heidi jumped out of bed and dressed herself with lightning speed. Then she ran down the ladder and outdoors to see what her clever grandfather would do next.

The night before, after the children had gone to bed, he had considered the problem of the wheel chair, and how to get it into the hut and under shelter. It could not be pushed in through the door for the opening was much too small. At last he decided to take two large boards off the big shutters from the shed, and thus he made an opening big enough for the chair to be pushed through into the workshop. Then he replaced the shutters without making them fast. Heidi scampered down just as her grandfather placed

Klara in her chair and rolled her out into the sunshine in front of the hut. He left her there and went to the great stalls. Heidi raced to her friend's side.

The fresh morning breeze brought the spicy perfume of the pines on every gust of air. Klara leaned back in her chair and drew in deep draughts of the delicious fragrance, and felt better than ever before in her whole life. She had never thought that life on the Alm could be like this.

"Oh, Heidi, I would love to live here always, always!" she said, turning her chair this way and that as she drank in the air and sunshine.

"Now you see that it is exactly as I told you it was," Heidi said. "The most beautiful spot in the whole world is at my grandfather's on the Alm!"

At that moment the grandfather came out of the goat-shed, with two mugs full of foaming, snow-white milk. One of these he gave to Klara, and the other to Heidi. "This is from Schwänli, and will give you lots of strength," he told Klara. "To your good health, child! Drink up!"

Klara had never tasted goat's milk before and she hesitated a little. But when she saw how eagerly Heidi drank hers, Klara decided to take a sip, and found it so sweet and spicy, as if sugar and nutmeg were mixed in it, that she emptied her mug at once.

"Tomorrow you will have two mugs," said the Uncle, with satisfaction.

Peter and his flock came up the Alm at the usual hour. While Heidi greeted the goats, the creatures managed to push her a little way up the hill with them.

The goatherd pressed in among the goats, saying, "You must come with us, Heidi."

"No, I can't," Heidi said, "Not for a long, long time. Not as long as Klara is with us. But my grandfather has promised that someday we will both go up." With this Heidi turned and twisted and got away from the goats and ran back to her friend.

Peter stared after her, scowling. Then he waved his rod

in the air until the goats took fright and fled up the mountain. The boy took after them, for all at once he bethought himself of the Alm-Uncle and of what *he* might think of the scowling and the rod waving, and decided to put some distance between them – fast.

But Klara and Heidi had planned so many things they might do today that they scarcely knew where to begin. First of all, Heidi suggested, they might write the daily letter promised to Grandmamma, in which they were to tell her exactly how everything went on the Alm. In that way the good lady would know at once if anything went wrong and if she were needed there. Otherwise she could continue her quiet stay in Ragatz.

"Must we go inside to write!" Klara asked, reluctant to leave the sights and sounds around her.

"No," Heidi said, and ran into the hut to bring out all her school materials for writing, together with the three-legged stool. She put her writing book on Klara's lap, so that she could write on it, and seated herself on the stool with the bench for a table, and they both began to write to the grandmamma.

But after every sentence that Klara wrote, she had to pause and look about. The wind softly fanned her face, and whispered to the pines. The lofty mountain peaks gazed down upon the valleys below. It was so beautiful, so beautiful, Klara thought.

The morning sped by and the grandfather came out with steaming bowls of dinner, for he said that Klara must stay out-of-doors as long as a ray of sunshine remained.

After their dinner Heidi rolled the wheel chair under the pines, for the children had decided to spend the afternoon in the cool shade, telling each other everything that had happened since Heidi left Frankfurt. So the day passed, and it was evening, and the goats came trotting down the mountainside, with a scowling goatherd behind them.

"Goodnight, Peter!" Heidi said when she saw that he did not mean to stop.

"Goodnight, Peter!" Klara called out, also.

But he gave no answer, and drove his goats along, without even a backward look for the girls.

When Klara spied the grandfather leading the pretty Schwänli to the stall to milk her, she was seized with such longing for the milk, that she could hardly wait to have it brought to her.

"This is strange, Heidi," she said quite astonished at herself. "For as long as I can remember, I have eaten only because I had to, and everything seemed to taste of cod liver oil. I've thought a thousand times, if only I didn't have to eat, ever! And now I can hardly wait for Grandfather with the milk!"

"Yes, I do understand," Heidi said, for she remembered her days in Frankfurt when she could scarcely swallow a morsel. Eating in the fresh mountain air was a very different matter, as Klara was finding out.

When the Alm-Uncle appeared with the two mugs, she took hers gratefully and drank it down even more quickly than Heidi usually did. Then she held out her mug to the grandfather and begged prettily, "Oh, please, may I have a little more?"

Eyes twinkling, he nodded and went off again. When he returned, he had the mugs topped with something else to eat, for during the afternoon he had walked over the green Maiensass, to the cow-keeper's cottage, where they made sweet yellow butter, and he had brought back a big round ball of it. Then he had cut two thick slices of bread and spread them generously with the butter for the children's supper. And now he stood and watched them eat away heartily, well pleased with their big appetites.

That night, when Klara went to bed, she did not lie awake and watch the stars. Instead, her blue eyes closed at once and she slept the night through in the most sound and restful sleep she had ever had.

So the next day passed, and the next. And then there came a great surprise for the girls. Two strong porters climbed the mountain, each carrying a brand new bed on his back. Everything to make the beds, including new white coverlets, came with them – and a letter from the grandmamma.

She wrote that the beds were for Heidi and Klara, and that Heidi was to take hers to Dorfli in the winter, because from now on she must sleep in a proper bed. The other bed could stay on the Alm for Klara, for her next visit. Then the grandmamma praised the girls for their long letters, and asked them to continue to write every day, so that she would know all that they did.

While the girls were reading the letter, the grandfather went upstairs and removed the covering from the hay beds and spread the hay about on the floor of the loft. Then, with the help of the men he carried the new beds up to the loft and set them up close together, so that the view through the round window might be the same from both pillows, for he knew how much it pleased the girls.

Klara loved her new life more and more every day, and she could not tell her grandmamma enough of the Uncle's kindness and care, and of how lively and amusing Heidi was – far more than in Frankfurt – and of how thankful she was to be on the Alm.

Since things were going so well, the grandmamma decided to postpone her visit to the Alm a while longer, for the steep mountain ride was no easy undertaking for her. The grandfather, she heard, took extraordinary interest in the small invalid, for no day passed that he did not think of something that might strengthen her. For example, Klara wrote that every afternoon he made long excursions among the rocks, going higher and higher, and brought back each time a bundle of sweet-scented herbs. This was forage for Schwänli, so that she might give ever more strengthening milk, and there were many other things that he did for Klara's comfort and happiness. The grandmamma was well content with the progress on the Alm.

It was now the third week of Klara's stay on the Alm.

For several mornings, now, when the Uncle had carried her down to her chair, he had said, "Won't you try to stand up just for a moment?"

Making a tremendous effort, Klara did try, to please him, but she always cried out at once, "Oh, it hurts so!" and clung to him for support. Nevertheless, every day he coaxed her to try a little longer and a little longer.

This was an especially lovely summer on the Alm. Every day the sun shone from cloudless skies, and flowers opened and spilled their perfume on the air; and every evening the sun threw a purple and rosy light over the rocky pinnacles and on the snow field opposite, and then vanished in a blazing sea of gold. Heidi told Klara about this over and over, for only in the high pasture was it possible to see this. There, on the great slopes, the shining golden heather-roses bloomed, and so many bluebells that it seemed as if the grass itself had grown blue, and nearby were whole bushes of brown flowers that smelled so sweet that one could scarcely get away if once one paused to enjoy them.

Her own accounts awakened such a longing in Heidi that she jumped up and ran to her grandfather at his workbench, exclaiming "Oh, Grandfather, can't we go to the pasture tomorrow? It's so beautiful up there now!"

"Very well," he said, "we'll go, but first Klara must do something for me. She must try standing up for me this evening."

Heidi ran back to Klara with the news, and Klara promised, at once, to try to stand on her feet as often as the Uncle wished. She was overjoyed at the thought of the trip to the beautiful goat pasture. And Heidi, too, was so excited that she shouted to Peter, as soon as she spied him coming down the mountain, "Peter! Peter! tomorrow we're going with you to stay all day!"

But the strange boy seemed no more pleased by this than by her telling him she could not go to the pasture with him. He scowled just as crossly and waved his rod as furiously over the innocent goats and clumped on down the hillside without a word.

That night, the girls went to their beautiful new beds with their heads so full of plans for the coming day, that they decided to stay awake all night and talk about them. But they had scarcely laid their heads on their pillows, before their chatter ceased abruptly and their eyes closed in sleep. Klara dreamed of a huge bluebell field; and Heidi seemed to hear the great old eagle calling, "Come! come! come!"

Chapter 23

A SURPRISE FROM KLARA

VERY early the next morning, just as the sun climbed over the mountain ridges and flooded the slopes with gold, the Uncle brought Klara's wheel chair out of the shop and placed it ready for the journey before the hut. Then he went up to the loft to wake the girls.

At this moment Peter came trudging into view. His goats no longer ran trustingly all about him up the mountain, for Peter was now in a constant bad temper and thrashed right and left with his rod, and where it hit, it hurt. He was now at the highest pitch of bitterness and anger. For weeks, he had not once had Heidi to himself. No matter how early he came up in the morning, the strange girl was always there in her chair, and Heidi had no eyes but for her. When he came down in the evening, there was the chair under the pine trees, and Heidi, with nothing more than a "Goodnight, Peter" for him. She had not gone once to the pasture with him through all these weeks, and now, today, she was coming, but the chair and the strange girl were coming too, and what good would that do him?

Peter knew exactly how it would be, and his inward fury

came to a boil when his eyes fell on the chair. It seemed to stare at him like a sly enemy.

The boy looked about him. Everything was quiet, no one in sight. Like a wild creature, he threw himself upon the chair and pushed it with all his strength towards the steepest part of the slope. Away flew the chair and vanished down the incline.

Peter rushed up the Alm as if he had suddenly taken wing. When he reached a big blackberry bush, he hid. He wanted to make sure the Uncle did not catch sight of him, and yet he was eager to see what would become of the chair. What a wonderful sight met his eyes! Far below, his enemy was plunging down faster and faster, now turning over, now making an awkward leap over a rock, then throwing itself down again on the earth, and rushing to its ruin. Bits and pieces of the chair flew in every direction.

Peter laughed and leaped about and stamped his feet in a wild dance of joy. Now surely the strange girl would have to go away, for she would have no means of moving about. Heidi would be alone again and would come with him to the pasture every day as she used to, and everything would be just as it was before. Peter did not yet begin to consider the consequences of his wicked act.

At that moment Heidi ran out of the house and turned towards the workshop. Behind her came the grandfather with Klara in his arms. Heidi looked about, ran around the corner, and came back again, very much puzzled.

"Where is the chair?" her grandfather asked.

"I'm looking for it, Grandfather. You told me that it was near the workshop," Heidi said, "but it isn't."

Meanwhile, the wind had grown stronger. It rattled the workshop door, and slammed it hard against the wall.

"Grandfather," Heidi exclaimed, "the wind has done it. Oh, dear! if the chair has rolled down to Dorfli, we can't get it back until it is too late for us to go to the pasture."

"If the chair has rolled down, there's no use getting it at all, for it has been broken into a hundred pieces," said

Grandfather, coming around the corner to look down the mountainside. "But how strange that it should have gone down," he added. He remembered where he had left it, and from there the chair would have had to go round the corner of the hut, before starting down the slope.

"Oh, what a shame! now we can't go today. Perhaps never," Klara said mournfully. "I shall have to go home, for I have no chair," and big tears gathered in her blue eyes.

But Heidi turned trustfully to her grandfather, and said, "Surely you can find some way for us to go up to the pasture today and to keep Klara here, too can't you, Grandfather?"

"We shall go up to the pasture, as we intended," said the Alm-Uncle, "and then we shall see what will happen next."

He went into the hut and brought out a pile of shawls, and put Klara down on them upon the sunny grass. Then he went to bring in the morning milk, and to bring Schwänli and Bärli from their shed.

As he did this, he wondered why the goatherd's whistle had not yet been heard that morning.

Then, taking Klara on one strong arm and the shawls and wraps on the other, he said, "There now, off we go! The goats can come with us."

This was entirely to Heidi's liking. One arm around Schwänli's neck and the other around Bärli's, she moved along behind her grandfather. The goats were so happy to be climbing the mountain with Heidi again that they pressed close to her all the way.

When the little party reached the pasture, they saw with surprise that the other goats were already there, feeding on the slopes in little groups. Young Peter was lying at his ease upon the grass, seemingly asleep.

"Well, sleepyhead," the Alm-Uncle said loudly, "and how is it that you passed us by this morning?"

At the sound of the well-known voice, Peter sprang to

his feet, but with his wits about him. "Nobody was up," he told the Uncle.

"Humph," said the Uncle. "Did you chance to see the chair as you went by?"

"What chair?" asked Peter, frowning.

The Uncle said no more, but spread out the shawls on the sunny slope, and set Klara down carefully upon them. "Are you comfortable?" he asked.

"As comfortable as if I were in my chair," she said and thanked him. "Oh, Heidi, this is the very nicest place," she added, looking all about.

The grandfather now prepared to go back. He told them to enjoy themselves, and when it was time, Heidi was to bring the dinner from the satchel that he had left over in the shade. Peter would get their milk, but Heidi must be sure that it came from Schwänli. Towards evening Grandfather would return, but now he must go down to see what had become of the wheel chair.

The sky was a deep blue, with not a single cloud seen in any direction. The great snow field above glittered in the sun as if diamonds covered it. The grey rock peaks stood high and firm, and the big eagle swooped below them, while the mountain wind blew cool upon the sunny Alm. The girls sat together, supremely happy. Now and again a goat came to lie down a little while beside them, the affectionate Snowball more often than some of the others.

Thus the time passed, and then Heidi thought of her favourite place where all the flowers grew. She longed to see if they were open, and as lovely as the year before. If she waited until the grandfather came up in the evening, the petals would be closed.

A bit doubtfully she asked, "Would you be angry, Klara, if I ran off a while and left you alone? I'd like so much to see how the flowers look – but wait, you need not be alone!" She sprang up and broke off several fine branches from the green bushes nearby. Then she led Snowball to Klara's side.

"There! now you'll have company," said Heidi, giving Snowball a little downward push. The pretty creature understood and lay down. Heidi put the branches into Klara's lap, and the invalid assured her that she did not mind being left alone with the friendly goat.

Heidi ran off, and Klara began to feed Snowball, leaf by leaf from a branch. Soon the small goat was quite tame, and nibbled the leaves delicately, one by one from Klara's hand. It was easy to see that the creature was happy there, for she did not go away, even when big Turk nudged her.

It delighted Klara to sit quietly thus, with the gentle goat looking up at her as if for protection. A great desire rose in the girl's heart to be for once mistress of herself, and able to help others. A longing to live always in the beautiful sunshine, and to do something that would give pleasure to others overwhelmed Klara. A new joy filled her heart, as if everything could be different and more beautiful, and all at once she had to hug the little goat about the neck and whisper in her ear, "Oh, Snowball, it is beautiful up here! If only I could stay here always!"

Meanwhile Heidi reached the flower field and gave a cry of delight, for the whole place was covered with blossoms – shining buttercups and clumps of bluebells that rocked to and fro, with the sweetest perfume coming from the little brown flowers which thrust their round heads here and there among the golden cups. Heidi stood still, drawing the scented air deep into her lungs. Suddenly she turned and raced back to Klara.

"Oh, you must see it all," she panted. "Everything is so beautiful! But all the petals close in the evening. Perhaps I can carry you!"

Klara stared at the excited Heidi, shaking her head.

"No, Heidi. How can you even think of it? You are much smaller than I. Oh, if I could only walk!"

Heidi never gave up easily. She cast about for some new idea.

Beyond the girls, on higher ground, Peter now sat staring

at them, as if he could not quite believe that they were there. He had destroyed the hateful chair so that the stranger would not be able to move – and here she was, sitting at Heidi's side. It was impossible, yet there she sat, and he could see her whenever he chose to turn his head.

Heidi disturbed that line of thought by calling to him. "Come down here, Peter!" she cried, her voice very decided.

"Won't come," he scowled.

"You must. I can't do it alone. I need your help. Hurry!" urged Heidi.

"Won't," he said again.

At this Heidi's temper flared. She ran up the mountain a little way and faced the lad with flaming eyes. "Peter, if you don't come this instant, I'll do something dreadful to you, and you may believe that!" she shouted.

These words brought Peter up quite short and filled him with anxiety. He had done something wicked – and secretly, he thought. He had even been pleased with himself up to this moment. But now Heidi was talking as if she knew all about it. What's more, she had as good as threatened to tell her grandfather, and Peter was more afraid of him than of any other person. If the Uncle should learn what had become of the chair! Peter grew more and more uneasy and without further argument, he rose and went to Heidi.

"I'm coming," he promised, "but then you must promise not to do it." He seemed so uneasy that Heidi took pity on him.

"All right, now I won't," she replied, not understanding his fright at all. "Come with me, and don't be afraid of what I want you to do."

When they reached Klara, Heidi told Peter to take the invalid firmly by one arm, while she herself held her by the other. In this way they could lift her up, she explained, and the plan succeeded. But now came the difficult part. Klara could not stand. How then could they hold her up and

178

bring her forward at the same time? Heidi was much too small to support Klara with her arm.

With her usual decision, Heidi gave the signal: "Now Klara! You must take me around the neck, quite firmly, so. Then you must take Peter's arm and hold fast to it. Then we can carry you."

Peter had never given anyone his arm before and when Klara took hold of it he merely allowed it to hang down stiffly by his side.

"That's not the way, Peter," Heidi said. "Curve your arm, and then Klara can put hers through it. She must lean on it with all her weight, and you must hold up steadily. Then we can move along nicely."

They did not make much progress, however. Klara was not light, and the pair supporting her were not well matched. On one side they went up and on the other down; so that the whole effort was most awkward and insecure.

Klara tried valiantly to move a little upon her own feet, but she drew them quickly up again.

"Put your foot straight down once," suggested Heidi, "and next time it won't hurt you so much."

"Do you really think so?" Klara asked doubtfully. She took the advice, however, and tested one firm step on the ground and then another, crying out a little at each step. Then she lifted a foot again, and set it down more carefully. "That didn't hurt me nearly as much," she exclaimed, delighted.

"Do it again," Heidi urged.

Klara did so again, and still again, and presently she cried out, "Heidi, I can! I can! Look! I can take steps, one after the other. Look!"

Heidi shouted so loudly for joy, that the echoes bounced back from the cliffs.

"Oh, Klara! Oh, Klara, can you really walk? Really truly? Oh, if Grandfather could see you! Now you can walk! Now you can walk!" she exclaimed over and over, quite beside herself with delight.

Klara held tight to the boy and girl, but at every step she became a little firmer, and gained more confidence. Heidi could scarcely contain herself.

"Now we can come up to the pasture every day, and go all over the Alm," she bubbled. "And you can walk on your own feet all your life, and need not be pushed about in your chair ever again. This is surely the most wonderful thing that could have happened."

Klara agreed with all her heart. Certainly there could be no greater happiness in the world than to feel well and strong, and to be able to go about like other people, and not be confined to an invalid's chair all day long.

It was not very far over to the flower field now. Heidi was already pointing out the glistening buttercups. Now they reached the clumps of bluebells and the inviting sunny patch of grass.

"Couldn't we sit down here?" Klara asked.

That was exactly what Heidi liked, and down they sat in the midst of the flowers. For the first time in her whole life Klara found herself seated on the soft warm grass. All around her were the swaying bluebells, the shining buttercups, the spicy wild plums. Everything was breathtakingly beautiful.

The two girls sat still for a long time, rejoicing in the new happiness that had come to them, their hearts quite full. The less sensitive Peter stretched out near them and fell asleep.

The time went by, and the sun was long past midday, when a small troop of goats came inquiringly up the flower covered slope. This was not their feeding place, for they did not like to graze in the flowers. They looked rather like a small search party, with Thistlebird in the lead. When he discovered the three missing human companions in the middle of the flowery slope, he gave a loud bleat, and then the whole flock came trotting towards the children.

The noise awakened Peter who sat up and rubbed his eyes hard, for he had dreamed that he saw the wheel chair standing before the hut door, safe and sound, with its red covering and every other part intact. Now his uneasiness returned, for although Heidi had promised not to do anything to him, the fear of discovery began to grow and grow within him. It made Peter very meek and willing to do everything Heidi asked of him.

Then the three children got back to the pasture again. Heidi hurried to the lunch bag intending to keep her promise faithfully, for it was in connection with the midday meal that she had threatened Peter. She had noticed how many good things her grandfather had put into the bag, and had been pleased to think of how Peter would like getting his share of them. Then, when he proved obstinate and disagreeable about helping Klara, she had threatened not to give him anything to eat. Peter, however, out of the guilt of his own conscience, had interpreted her words quite differently. All unknowing, Heidi divided the contents of the bag into three generous piles, smiling all the while with satisfaction.

Giving each his portion, she settled herself by Klara's side, and the two girls enjoyed their dinner enormously after their unusual exertions. Peter ate his large portion quietly, down to the last crumb, but not with his usual appetite. Something weighed on him, and made his food stick in his throat.

The children had come down for their dinner so late that soon after they had eaten, the grandfather came up the Alm for them. Heidi flew to meet him, for she wished to be the first to tell him what had occurred, but she was so excited over her news that she could hardly find words with which to tell it. However he soon understood what she meant, and with great delight hastened to Klara.

"So now," he said, "we have really tried, and really succeeded."

He raised Klara from the ground gently, placed his left arm around her waist, and held his right out as a firm support for her hand, and Klara walked, more surely than before, with his steady support. Heidi jumped up and down, clapping her hands for joy, and the Uncle looked as if some extraordinary good fortune had come his way. He soon lifted Klara off her feet, however, saying, "We must not overdo things the first time, but get you home." And he at once set himself to the task, for he knew that now Klara needed rest as soon as possible.

That evening when Peter came down to Dorfli with the flock, a large crowd of villagers were gathered together, pushing each other for a better view of what was lying on the ground. The curious Peter at once elbowed his way through the crowd.

And there it was. There on the grass lay the mid-section of the wheel chair, with a part of the back still hanging on crookedly. The red covering and the shining brass nails showed what a handsome chair it must have been.

"I was here when it came, to be carried up the Alm," the baker declared, "It was worth a pretty penny, I'll wager. I'd certainly like to know how it happened."

"The wind must have rolled it down. The Uncle himself said so," Barbel nodded wisely as she fingered the red covering.

"It is a lucky thing that no one else did it," the baker said. "He would catch it, surely. When the gentleman in Frankfurt finds out, he will look into the matter. For my part, I am glad that I have not been upon the Alm these two years past. Suspicion certainly will fall on anyone who has been up there lately."

Other opinions were put forth, but Peter had heard quite enough. He crept out of the crowd, and ran with all his speed up the Alm, as if someone were already after him. The baker's voice had terrified him. At any moment a policeman might come from Frankfurt, to investigate the matter, and then it would come out that he was guilty, and they would seize him and send him to the house of correction. Peter saw this so clearly that his hair stood on end.

By the time the boy reached home, he was completely

unnerved. He would answer no questions, he would not eat his dinner – and he crept to his bed as fast as he could, and lay there groaning.

"Peterkin must have been eating sorrel again," said his mother, Brigitte. "He has a terrible stomach-ache. Hear how he moans and groans."

"You must give him more bread to take with him. Give him a piece of my roll tomorrow," said the grandmother pityingly.

When the two girls looked from their beds out into the starlit heavens that same night, Heidi said, "Have you realized, Klara, what a good thing it is that God does not grant our prayers, if He has something better in store for us?"

"Why do you say that now?" Klara asked.

"Don't you know how hard I prayed in Frankfurt that I might go home right away? And when the good God did not let me go, I thought that He had not listened to my prayers. But you see, if I had gone away then, you would never have come here, and you would not have learned to walk on the Alm."

Klara grew thoughtful. "How did you think all this out, Heidi?" she asked.

"Your grandmamma explained it all to me first, and then it happened just as she said, and I knew it was true. Today we ought to thank the dear God especially for the great joy He has sent us in showing you how to walk."

"Yes, Heidi, you are right. I'm glad you have reminded me. Out of sheer happiness I had forgotten."

So the children bowed their heads and prayed, and thanked the Lord for curing Klara who had been an invalid for so long.

The next morning the grandfather suggested that the girls should write to the grandmamma in Ragatz, and ask her to come up to the Alm, as there was something new to see there. But they had a plan of their own. They thought it would make a great surprise if Klara were to practise first until she could walk supported by Heidi alone. In the meantime, the grandmamma was to have no inkling of the wonderful news. How long did the Uncle think it would take?

"Not more than a week," he said. So then they decided to write, inviting the grandmamma urgently to be on the Alm at the end of a week. But not a hint of the surprise did they give.

The days that followed were the happiest of all for Klara. Every morning she awakened with the happy knowledge ringing in her heart: "I can walk! I can walk!"

The exercises followed, and Klara felt stronger with each one, and took a longer walk each day. The extra activity brought such an appetite, that daily the slice of bread and butter had to be made bigger, and the grandfather stood by and watched it vanish with immense satisfaction. And always there was a big jug of the foaming milk which also disappeared as if by magic. At last the week went by, and the day came when the grandmamma was expected on the Alm!

Chapter 23

GOODBYE FOR A WHILE

A DAY before she was to start, the grandmamma sent off a letter to the Alm, so that they would know exactly when to expect her. Peter brought this letter with him, on the way to the pasture.

The Alm-Uncle and the girls were already out in front of the hut, with Schwänli and Bärli, waiting for the goatherd.

When Peter saw the group his pace slowed considerably. Finally, since he could not avoid it, he held the letter out to the Uncle, and the moment it left his hand he jumped back, looking behind him quickly, as if something fearful might be there. Then with a bound he took off, up the mountain.

"Grandfather," said Heidi, much puzzled by this queer conduct, "why does Peter behave exactly like big Turk, when he sees a rod behind him?"

"Perhaps Peter also sees a rod behind him, and one that he deserves," replied her grandfather.

By this time, the lad was out of sight of the hut. Then he stopped and turned his head about, in every direction, jumping at every movement, for it seemed to him that Frankfurt policemen were hiding behind every bush, ready to spring upon him. This apprehension never left him, and Peter grew more and more anxious and unhappy. In fits and starts he made his way up to the pasture, and finally collapsed behind some concealing rocks.

Having read Grandmamma's letter, the girls went inside the hut, where Heidi at once began to put everything in order, for the grandmamma must find everything just so. The morning slipped away and it was almost time for their visitor's arrival before they knew it.

Then they came out and seated themselves on the bench to await the lady. But sitting still never agreed with Heidi, so every little while up she jumped to peer down the slope for the first sign of their visitor.

At long last there was the procession, winding up the mountain. First the guide, then the grandmamma on the white horse, and then the porter with a basket piled high with all sorts of things. Nearer and nearer they came, until the grandmamma reached the summit and caught sight of the girls.

"Klara!" she cried. "What do I see? You are not in your chair!" Excited, Grandmamma hastened to dismount, but even as she did this, she went on exclaiming. "Is this really you, Klara? Your cheeks are round and apple-red. Dear child, I scarcely know you!"

Before the good lady could run to her grandchild, Heidi sprang up, and Klara rose also, steadying herself on her small friend's shoulder. Then the two girls calmly walked towards the grandmamma, while the poor lady stood still with fright, thinking that Heidi was trying something rash.

She could not believe her eyes. Klara was walking by Heidi's side! And both girls were looking at the grandmamma with faces beaming. Now the grandmamma ran to meet them. Laughing and crying all at once, she held Klara in her arms, then Heidi, and then again her granddaughter. She had no words to express her joy.

Presently she saw the Uncle, observing the excited group with a contented smile. The grandmamma took Klara by the arm, and with increasing wonder and delight moved with her towards the bench. Then seating Klara, she seized the Uncle's hands.

"My dear, good Uncle! How can we ever thank you? This is your work, I know. Your care and nursing–"

"And the good Lord's sunshine and mountain air," the Uncle added, smiling.

"Yes, and Schwänli's milk, too," Klara added. "You must see me drinking the goat's milk. Grandmamma. It is so good!"

The grandmamma's eyes misted with happiness. "I really do not know you, Klara. You have grown round and plump, and more rosy than I ever dreamed you could be. Dear child, dear child. We must not lose a moment, but telegraph to your Papa in Paris. He must come to see you at once! We won't tell him why, for this will be the greatest happiness of his whole life. How can we manage this, dear Uncle? Have the men gone already?"

"Yes, they are gone, but we can send the goatherd down with the message. I will call him."

The Uncle went behind the hut and gave a piercing whistle through his fingers, so that the echo came back from the rocks far above. It soon brought Peter down, on the run, white as chalk, for he thought that the Uncle was whistling him down for punishment, and since there was no way to avoid it, he might as well come down and take it – now.

Instead only a bit of paper was given him, which the grandmamma had just written, and he was told to take it down to the post office in Dorfli. Peter set out quite relieved, clutching the paper in his hand. The Uncle had not whistled him down to be punished, and no policeman from Frankfurt was to be seen. All was well – so far.

The party now seated themselves at the table, and they told the grandmamma everything that had happened, from the very beginning. The telling took a long time, for the grandmamma interrupted constantly with questions, and exclamations of thankful surprise.

"And now," Grandmamma said finally, "my weak and pale little invalid is changed into this radiant darling! It's like a fairy tale, it is indeed, and such a wonderful surprise."

Meanwhile, Mr. Sesemann also was planning a surprise. He had been seized with an irresistible longing to see his daughter, from whom he had been separated all summer. So one fine morning he set out from Paris, arriving in Ragatz just after his mother had left for the Alm. He had followed by carriage to Mayenfeld, and then on to Dorfli, from where he intended to walk up the Alm.

Wasting no time in Dorfli, he started the climb at once. Presently he saw that there were footpaths everywhere, crossing and recrossing each other. Mr. Sesemann began to wonder if he were following the right one. He looked about, hoping to find someone to ask. And providentially, someone was running down the mountain.

It was Peter, with his message in his hand. He ran, however, as the crow flies, following no path but the one of least resistance. As soon as he came within hailing distance, Mr. Sesemann called to him and Peter stopped dead in his tracks.

"Come here, boy. This way!" Mr. Sesemann beckoned encouragingly, but the lad now dragged his feet and edged along crabwise. "Just tell me if I'm on the right path to a mountain cottage where an old man lives with a child named Heidi, whom the people from Frankfurt are visiting," Mr. Sesemann asked.

A look of horror crossed Peter's face and he clapped a hand to his mouth, smothering a cry. The next second he had dashed away, but with such tremendous force that he turned head over heels and rolled down the slope, very much as the wheel chair had done some days before. Only fortunately for Peter, he did not fall to pieces. His only loss was the message, which slipped from his grasp and flew away.

"An unusually shy mountain lad," Mr. Sesemann murmured, watching Peter's departure with astonishment. "Probably not used to strangers." As the boy vanished round a bend, Mr. Sesemann continued his upward climb – hoping for the best, hoping the boy would not be hurt, and hoping that he himself was on the right track.

Peter could not stop his headlong plunge, no matter how he tried. He rolled on and on, and now and then turned an involuntary somersault. But this experience was nothing, compared to the knowledge that the policeman had at last arrived from Frankfurt. Peter did not doubt for a moment that the stranger asking the way to the Alm-Uncle's hut was he. At last the goatherd tumbled into a bush, halfway down the last slope to Dörfli, and there he stuck fast, trying to collect himself and think what to do next.

"Well, now! here comes another," said a voice close by. "And who will get a shove tomorrow, I wonder, and come tumbling down like a sack of potatoes?"

It was the Dörfli baker, joking thus at Peter's plight. He had come up the Alm a little way, to refresh himself after his hot day's work at the ovens, and had watched Peter roll, not unlike the wheel chair, end over end, down the steep mountainside.

The lad scrambled to his feet, a new fear upon him. Now the baker knew, also, that the chair had been pushed down and not by the wind! Without a backward glance Peter turned up the mountain again.

He would have much preferred to creep into his bed, for he felt safest there, but his goats were still above, and the uncle had ordered him to come back quickly, because they should not be left alone very long. Peter had never yet ventured to disobey the Uncle. So now he groaned and limped on, feeling every one of his bruises all the way up the Alm.

Mr. Sesemann was on the right track after all. He reached the first cottage soon after he had seen Peter, and then at last there was the Alm-hut, with the dark treetops of the old pines waving to and fro above it.

By this time he had been discovered and recognized by the party out in front of the hut, and though his arrival was a surprise, the surprise awaiting him was even greater. As he came up the last slope, two figures came towards him – a tall girl, with fair hair and a rosy face, supporting herself upon the smaller but beaming Heidi.

Mr. Sesemann started, feeling a clutch at his heart, and then the sting of tears in his eyes. For a moment he did not know whether he was awake or asleep.

"Papa, don't you know me? Am I that different?"

But with these words Klara was clasped in her father's arms. "Yes, you are different! Is it possible? I cannot believe it!" The father stepped back, to see if the picture would vanish from before his eyes, and when it did not, he again folded Klara in his arms. Then he held her off from him, to inspect her rosy cheeks and her lovely straight bearing, and the legs which now could walk.

The grandmamma went to her son now and kissed him affectionately. "Is it not a blessed miracle?" she said. "But now you must come and meet the Uncle, who is our great benefactor."

"To be sure, Mother, and I ought to say a word to our little friend, also," said Mr. Sesemann, taking Heidi's hand. "I need not ask how you are, for I can see you're fresh and healthy once more on the Alm. No Alpine rose could look more blooming. This is a great joy to me, child, a great joy."

Heidi looked affectionately into Mr. Sesemann's face. He had always been so good to her! How wonderful that now she had some part in this great happiness.

Mr. Sesemann turned to the Alm-Uncle, to give him his heartfelt thanks, and the grandmamma decided to leave the two men alone for the time being. So she and the girls strolled out under the pines.

And there, under the great branches she found a bouquet of wonderful dark blue gentians. She clasped her hands with pleasure.

"How lovely! Dear Heidi, did you pick these for me?"

"No," Heidi said, "but I know who did."

A rustling behind the pines turned the grandmamma's attention that way. It was Peter. He had made a wide circle, to creep secretly along under the trees to see what the "policeman" from Frankfurt was doing at the Alm-hut.

The grandmamma recognized him, and had a new thought: Peter must have brought the flowers down for her, and now was hiding himself from pure bashfulness. That could not be permitted, for he must have a reward.

"Come, my lad, come quickly. Don't be afraid!" said the grandmamma, waving Peter in to her.

The boy stood paralyzed with fear. Escape was no longer possible. All was known. Trembling from head to foot, he crept out from behind the pines.

"Come, boy, don't stay there," the grandmamma urged. "And tell me, did you do it?"

As Peter had his eyes tightly shut, he did not see where the lady was pointing. And when he did venture to open them a bit, he saw that the Uncle was standing at the corner of the hut, piercing him with his eyes, and that the dreadful policeman from Frankfurt was right there by his side. Trembling in every limb Peter cried loudly, "Yes!"

"My boy," said the grandmamma, "why do you look so frightened?"

"Because," wailed Peter, "it is all broken in pieces, and can never be mended."

To the grandmamma, the boy appeared ready to fly apart himself. She went hurriedly to the corner of the hut and said, "My dear Uncle, is this lad right in the head?"

"I sometimes wonder," said the Uncle severely. "You see the boy is also the wind that pushed the wheel chair down the mountain, and now he is fearful of his well-earned punishment."

The grandmamma could scarcely believe this, for Peter did not look mischievous. Besides, what reason would he have for destroying something so useful as the wheel chair?

The Uncle stared hard at Peter, for indeed, he had had only a suspicion to sustain his accusation. But it was a suspicion born directly after the deed. The scowling looks that Peter had directed at Klara from the very first, and all the other signs of dislike he had displayed towards the visitors to the Alm, had not escaped the Uncle. He had put this and that together, and was quite certain that he had the story, which he now related to the astonished grandmamma, and recommended a sound chastisement for the lad.

When he had finished, the lady shook her head vigorously. "No, my dear Uncle, no. The poor lad has been punished enough already. We must be merciful and understanding. Think how you might feel in his place! Here come strange people from Frankfurt and carry off his Heidi for weeks at a time, while he sits up on the lonely mountain slopes day after day, and looks on. We must be forgiving. Anger has driven him to a revenge – a stupid one, it's true, but anger makes all of us stupid."

Whereupon the grandmamma went over to the still trembling Peter and sat down on the bench under the pines, saying kindly, "Come here, boy, I want to talk to you. Stop shaking so and listen. You did push the wheel chair down the mountain, to break it in pieces. That was wicked, and you knew it. That you deserved to be punished, you knew also, and so you hoped very hard that no one would find out what you had done.

"But you see, whoever does a wrong deed, and thinks that no one knows it, only deceives himself. God sees and hears everything, and He at once wakens in the wrongdoer the little watchman, that he has placed in everybody at his birth. This little watchman is allowed to sleep until that person has done something wrong. The watchman has a small goad in his hand, and with this he keeps pricking the wrongdoer, until he has not one moment's peace. And on top of this, he keeps crying out, 'It's all found out! They are coming to punish you!' Have you felt something like this, Peter?"

The lad nodded, quite stunned, for that was exactly how it had been with him.

"And yet, in one way, you were disappointed," the grandmamma went on, "because the wrong thing that you did turned out to be the very best for the person you wished to harm. When Klara had no chair in which she could be carried up the mountain to see the lovely pasture and the flowers, she made a great effort to get to them. And thus she learned to walk, and now she walks better and better every day. If she were to stay here, at last she would be able to go to the pasture whenever she chose. Much oftener than if she had to be carried up.

"So you see, Peter, God can turn anything that is meant to be harmful into something good for the person who was to be hurt. Only the wrongdoer injures himself. Do you understand, Peter? Well, then, think it over, and whenever you have a desire to do something wrong, think of the little watchman inside of you with his annoying voice. Will you promise me to do that?"

"Yes, I will," replied Peter. But he was more depressed than ever. He had no idea how all this would end, for there was the policeman, standing all this time beside the Uncle and looking at him.

"Well, then, that is good," said the grandmamma, "and the matter is settled. But now I want to give you something nice to help you remember the people from Frankfurt. Tell me, what have you wished for very much? What would you like to have?"

At this, Peter's head came up and he stared at the grandmamma with big round eyes. He had been expecting something dreadful to happen to him, but now the good lady was offering to give him something that he wanted very much! He did not know what to think of such a turn of events.

"I am quite in earnest," said the grandmamma, "you shall see. Only tell me of something that you will like very much, to remind you of us, and to show you that we forgive you. Don't you understand, my boy?"

Peter's head began to clear a little, and he understood that he had no punishment to fear. In fact, this lady had as much as promised to save him from the policeman. He felt as if a mountain had been lifted from his back. He also understood that it was wiser to confess at once to something done wrong than to wait until it was found out, so he took a deep breath and blurted out, "And I lost the paper, too."

The grandmamma had to knit her brows over this announcement, but at last she discovered the connection, and said kindly, "It is good of you to tell it, Peter. Always confess anything you have done that is wrong, and then it can be settled quickly and less harm done. Now tell me what would you like to have?"

To be given leave to choose anything in the world, left Peter quite dizzy. The whole Fair at Mayenfeld swam before his eyes, with all the beautiful things that he had always looked at and never even hoped to possess. Peter's fortune never exceeded a penny, and at the Fair everything cost at least double. There were the fine red whistles, which he could use for his goats! and there were handsome knives with round handles; and – oh, lots and lots of wonderful things.

So he said, quite decidedly, "Two francs."

The grandmamma threw her head back and laughed.

"That is very modest. Come here!"

She opened her purse, and took from it a crisp crackly note to which she added four francs. "Now," she said "here we have as many two francs as there are weeks in the year. You can take two francs out to use every Sunday, and so have a bit every week the year round."

"All the rest of my life?" asked Peter, wonderingly. He had never been strong on arithmetic.

At this the grandmamma began to laugh so hard that the Uncle and Mr. Sesemann stopped talking in order to hear what was going on.

"You shall have it, my lad," said the grandmamma, still laughing. "I shall have it put in my will – do you hear, my son? Two francs a week to goat-Peter, as long as he lives."

Mr. Sesemann nodded approvingly, and turned away, his shoulders shaking. The laughter did not bother Peter one whit. He had eyes for nothing but the money in his hand. It was reassuringly solid and real. A loud "Thank God!" burst from him, and then he ran off in extraordinary, joyful leaps, all fear and anxiety gone, and the prospect of two francs every week for all the rest of his life, setting wings to his feet.

Later in the day, when the merry party on the Alm had finished their outdoor midday dinner, and sat talking at their ease, Klara took her father's hand, saying, "Oh, Papa, if you could only know what the dear grandfather has done for me every single day that I have been up here. It would be impossible to tell it all, but I shall never forget, and shall always be thinking of how I can do something for him, or send him a present, that will make him half as happy as he has made me."

"This is my wish, also, dearest child," replied her father.

"At this very moment I am trying to decide how we can in some small measure, repay what we owe to his kindness."

Mr. Sesemann patted his daughter's hand and then went to the Uncle, who was talking with the grandmamma.

"My dear friend," said Mr. Sesemann, placing his arm affectionately round the old man, "I'm certain you know that for many years I haven't known real happiness. What could money or business success mean to me when I looked at my child and realized that nothing could buy her health? Through the Lord's guidance, I feel that you have healed my daughter, given her, and me, also, a new and wonderful life. How can I show my gratitude? I know I can never repay you in full, but whatever I have I put at your disposal. You have only to name it, and it is yours."

The Alm-Uncle looked at the father with kindly eyes. Then he said, "Your child's recovery has given me great pleasure, too, Mr. Sesemann. I feel I've had my reward. I thank you for your offer, but I need nothing now for myself or for my grandchild. I have one wish, however, and should it be fulfilled, I would have no further concern in this life."

"Only name it, dear friend," Mr. Sesemann begged.

"I am old," the Uncle said, "and I cannot live for many more years. When I go, there is nothing I can leave Heidi, and the only other relative she has cannot be trusted with the child's best interests."

To that Mr. Sesemann nodded, for he had met Dete and understood her perfectly.

"Therefore," the old man continued, "if you would give me the assurance that my Heidi will never need to go out among strangers to earn her living, I will be most richly repaid for whatever I may have done for Klara, and everlastingly grateful to you for my peace of mind."

"My dear friend," cried Mr. Sesemann, "there can never be any question of that. Heidi belongs to us. Ask my mother and my daughter! Heidi shall never need to seek comfort amongst strangers. Here is my hand on it, and my solemn promise. I will see to it now and, through my will, provide for her later, also. Moreover, we all know that Heidi should not live away from her mountains, no matter how fine the circumstances might be. And, she has other friends aware of this.

"There is such a one in Frankfurt now, who is settling his affairs so as to be able to go where he pleases. This is our friend, Dr. Classen, who intends to return here in the autumn. He wishes to establish himself in this vicinity, after taking counsel with you, for he has never felt more welcome or at ease anywhere else. So you see, Heidi will have two protectors near her, and may they both be with her for a long, long time."

At this, the grandmamma took the Uncle's hand with great affection, and then put her arm round Heidi, saying tenderly, "And you, dear child, you also must ask for something we can give you. Tell me, what is your dearest wish?"

Heidi looked at the grandmamma delightedly, and then all in one breath, she said, "I'd like to have my bed from Frankfurt with the three high pillows and the warm coverlet, because then the blind grandmother could lie with her head well up and be able to breathe, and not be cold and have to be wrapped in a shawl and stay in her hard little bed because it is so cold in goat-Peter's cottage."

"My dear Heidi!" exclaimed the grandmamma, so moved that tears sprang to her eyes. "It is well that you have reminded me of the blind grandmother, for in my own great happiness I did not think of her. Forgive me, dear child. We shall telegraph to Frankfurt at once, and this very day Rottenmeier shall pack the bed. It will be here in two days. The grandmother shall sleep well in it."

Clapping her hands, Heidi danced round and round the grandmamma. But all at once she stopped. "I must go down to tell Grandmother all about it," she said, "for she will be anxious to know what has been going on. I have not visited her for a long time."

"No, Heidi. What are you thinking off?" reproved her

grandfather. "We have guests and it would not be proper for you to run off and leave them."

But the grandmamma agreed with Heidi. "My dear Uncle, the child is right," said she. "The poor grandmother has been deprived of Heidi's company long enough on our account. We'll all go together to see her, and I'll take my horse from her cottage. Then we shall go down to Dorfli, and telegraph to Frankfurt. What do you think of this, my son?"

But Mr. Sesemann had plans of his own – and some that were newly made. He therefore begged his mother to wait a bit while he discussed them.

He had intended to travel with his mother through Switzerland, and to see if Klara were strong enough to go a short distance with them. Now all was different, for he could have a real tour with his daughter, all through these beautiful late summer days. He therefore thought he would spend the night in Dorfli, and the next day he could then take Klara away from the Alm to join her grandmamma in Ragatzbad, where they could start on their tour.

Klara and Heidi looked distressed at this sudden prospect of parting, but there was so much else to be happy about, that they faced it bravely.

With all decided, the grandmamma rose and took Heidi's hand, ready to start on their visit, when she remembered her granddaughter. "What shall we do with Klara?" she asked. "The walk to goat-Peter's cottage will be far too long for her."

"That can be solved most easily," the Uncle said, and taking Klara on his arm, he followed the happy grandmamma and Heidi, with Mr. Sesemann bringing up the rear.

Heidi went skipping along at the grandmamma's side, answering her questions about the poor blind woman. How did she live, the grandmamma asked, and how were things managed in her house, especially in the cold winter? Heidi could answer fully, for she knew how the poor grandmother sat huddled in her corner, shivering with cold, and what she had to eat, and what she had not.

The grandmamma listened most attentively, and soon they came in sight of the cottage.

Brigitte just then was hanging Peter's second shirt on a bush to dry. When she saw the company, and all going down the mountain, she ran into the cottage.

"Now they are all going away together, Mother," she exclaimed. "There is a whole procession of them, and the Uncle is carrying the sick one."

"Oh, must this really happen?" sighed the grandmother. "Are they taking Heidi with them? Did you see? Oh, if I could only hear her voice again!"

At this moment the cottage door flew open, and Heidi rushed in and went straight to the corner where the old woman sat, and flung her arms about her. "Grandmother! What do you think? My bed is coming from Frankfurt, with all three pillows, and the warm coverlet. They will be here in two days. Klara's grandmamma says so." Heidi's words tumbled joyously, one over the other as she watched for the expression of delight to come upon the old grandmother's face. But, though she smiled, the old woman still look rather sad.

"Oh what a good lady!" she said. "I ought to be glad that she is taking you with her, Heidi, but I don't know how I shall live through it."

"What? And who said anything like that?" asked Mrs. Sesemann, taking the hand of the blind grandmother and pressing it warmly. "There is no such plan afoot, I can assure you. Heidi is going to stay right here on the Alm and make everyone happy. It is we who shall come up to the Alm every year, for we have good reason to thank God for the blessing He has given us up here."

At these words, a true happiness came over the face of the blind grandmother, while two big tears of gratitude rolled slowly down her cheeks.

Heidi nestled closely to the old woman, her own young heart full on the grandmother's account.

Mrs. Sesemann watched the tender scene for a time and then said gently. "I must bid you farewell now, Grandmother, for it is time for us to go. But we shall meet again before too long, as we are returning next year, and we are going to visit you then." She took the old, worn hand in hers and shook it kindly, with many other words of cheer and good will.

Klara's father and grandmamma then went down into the valley, while the Uncle picked up Klara as if she were a feather, and started up the Alm once more. Heidi gambolled ahead and alongside like one of the little goats whom she loved.

But next morning there were floods of tears when it was time for Klara to take leave of Heidi and the Alm-Uncle. It was not easy to leave the beautiful mountains, and the dear little hut where she had been so happy, and all the other pleasant remembered things.

Gulping back her own tears, Heidi said as cheerily as she could, "It will be summer again almost before we know it, and then you will come back, and it will be more beautiful than ever. And by that time you will be really strong and we'll be able to go about everywhere together."

At these words, Klara brightened, although she still held on to Heidi's hand tightly.

Mr. Sesemann had come, as agreed, to take his daughter. While he stood talking with the grandfather, Klara wiped her eyes, and with a little sniff said, "Say goodbye to Peter for me, and all the goats, too. I wish there were something I could give Schwänli. She helped so much to make me well and strong."

"You can! and very easily, too," said Heidi. "Just send her a little salt. You know how much she likes to lick it from Grandfather's hand in the evening."

"Heidi, you think of everything," exclaimed Klara, "I'll

do that very thing. I'll send a hundred pounds from Frankfurt!"

Mr. Sesemann now beckoned to the children, for it was time to go. The grandmamma's white horse had been sent up for Klara; she could ride down, as she no longer needed a sedan chair.

The girls embraced, and Klara was lifted into the saddle. Heidi ran to a high point from which she could see a good part of the slope, and waved her hand to Klara until there was not so much as a speck of the horse or rider to be seen.

The bed from Frankfurt arrived two days after Klara and her father left the Alm, and ever since the grandmother has slept soundly in it, rising every morning with new strength for the day. The good grandmamma also remembered what Heidi told her of the hard winters on the mountain, and so she also sent on a big box of all sorts of warm things to goat-Peter's cottage. Now the grandmother can wrap herself snugly whenever she wishes and she has no fear of the cold in her corner. She does not feel it!

In Dorfli a great building is going up, for the doctor has come from Frankfurt and bought the old mansion in which Heidi and the grandfather spent the winter. The fine room with the stove and the picture tiles, and other quarters also, are being kept as lodgings for the grandfather. But the rest is being rebuilt for the doctor, himself. Schwänli and Bärli have not been forgotten, either, for they will have comfortable winter stalls at the back of the great new house.

The doctor and the Alm-Uncle grow more friendly every day as they inspect the progress of the rebuilding. But mostly they talk of Heidi, whom they both love, and how happy she will be in the new dwelling – and they with her.

"My dear friend," said the doctor one day as they stood together in the courtyard, "here is my point of view on this situation. Since I share all your pleasure in the child, as if I, too, were her next of kin, I must also share the responsibilities, and help decide as to what is best for her welfare.

In this way I can earn a right to our Heidi, and can hope that she will care for me in my old age as a daughter might have done. That is my dearest wish, Uncle. She shall be named and recognized as my heiress, and when you and I leave her behind, neither of us will need to be anxious as to her comfort. She will be more than well provided for."

The Uncle pressed the doctor's hand silently, his eyes moist with emotion, for his heart was deeply stirred.

In the meantime, back on the Alm, Heidi and Peter sat at the grandmother's side, while the old woman listened intently to the little girl's chatter of all the exciting events of the past summer, which had kept her from making her usual visits to her old friend. And Peter's mother, Brigitte, bustled about nearby.

Of all the faces, perhaps hers was the happiest, for now at last she had learned the truth concerning her son's miraculous two francs, which had puzzled her no end up to now, and Heidi's explaining of the matter.

The grandmother put a hand on the excited Heidi's arm and said, "Read me a hymn of praise, child. It seems to me that we ought to do nothing but thank and glorify the Lord for all the good things He has brought into our lives – all of which, it seems to me, began with Heidi's coming to live with the Alm-Uncle."

Before she was through speaking, Heidi was up and reaching for the old hymnbook, just as she had done many times before, and would, many times again.